THE BILLIONAIRESS' COWBOY

BILLIONAIRE HEARTS RANCH BOOK 2

EDITH MACKENZIE

The Billionairess' Cowboy (Billionaire Hearts Ranch Book #2):

Images © DepositPhotos – Alan Poulson & dibrova. Cover Design © Designed with Grace

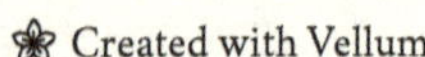 Created with Vellum

For the little girl I was, the dreams I had. When no one believed in you, I did. And I still do.

PROLOGUE

It was always the same. Loud and harshly spoken words flying around the house, the weapons of choice her parents chose when dealing with yet another upheaval her brother had caused. This time it was about money he'd stolen from them. Dad threatened it was the final straw. Mom would soon be pleading for her son, believing it all to be yet another misunderstanding, that he means to pay it back. From where Misty was standing, they were both equally delusional.

She closed the door behind her soundlessly. It's not like they'd have noticed if she'd slammed it. There wasn't much she could do that would focus their attention on her these days. Not having just sat her final high school exam a mere three months after she'd turned sixteen. Nor the fact that her school counselor was confident that she should be able to get a full scholarship to her college of choice. Nope. None of that was worthy of her parents' attention. It wasn't that they meant to ignore her, it was just that there was nothing left for her after her brother, Brandon, was finished draining the tank.

It didn't matter, Misty decided as she headed down the street toward her school, the late afternoon sun casting long shadows in front of her. Nothing was going to ruin her Friday night. Tonight, she'd sit in the bleachers with her best friends, Evelyn and Indie. They'd gossip and cheer as the team played. Indie's big brother, Colt, was playing and so was her boyfriend, Bennett. But she wasn't the only one to have someone to cheer on. Over the past few months, Colt's best friend, Logan had been paying particular attention to Misty. He was cute and the star quarterback. She still had to pinch herself that he'd even noticed her. But lately, whenever she was over at Evelyn's house, Logan had seemed to have found a reason to be there too, telling her how pretty she looked or telling her a joke just to make her smile.

Misty waved, smiling brightly when she spotted her friends already in position. Happily, she bounded up to join them. There was going to be a party after the game at the lake tonight, and Logan had asked if she was going. When she'd said she wasn't sure, he'd said he hoped to see her there. She sighed dreamily. Logan saying he wanted to see her at a party. Her stomach fluttered at the thought of what the night might bring. At sixteen she still hadn't been kissed, but when she practiced in the mirror, it was always Logan she pictured.

"I love how cute Bennett looks in his football uniform," Indie said, waving at her boyfriend, a gesture he was quick to return, blowing her a kiss.

"Yeah, there's something about it," agreed Evelyn, eyeing Colt. Misty had her suspicions about her friend's feeling for Indie's older brother. Not that Evelyn had ever said anything. She was always nose deep in art books and talking about going to London and living as an artist. It all sounded very romantic, but not very practical if you asked her. Misty knew exactly what she planned to do. She was going to be rich and get the heck away from her parents' arguing and her brother's manipulations. And her brains—that was her ticket to freedom.

"Misty, are you going to the party?" Indie leaned across Evelyn, her eyes glowing with excitement. "You can get a lift with me and Bennett. Evelyn's already coming with us."

"Yeah, but I have a ride." Misty gazed out at Logan tossing the ball, warming up. He looked up briefly, setting her heart thumping painfully in her chest, before the coach called them in to a huddle. This was going to be a night to remember.

After what felt like the world's longest football game, Misty scampered down the bleachers with her friends to wait for the boys. Bennett was the first to appear, picking Indie up and twirling her about, her hair fanning out behind her as she giggled in delight. Colt rolled his eyes when he saw it.

"Don't make me come over there and have you put my sister down."

Evelyn laughed, looking between the two of them. Although Colt was over six foot, Bennett was much broader. "I'm not sure you could."

"I'd give it a fair try," Colt growled good-naturedly.

Misty looked around. Logan still hadn't appeared. Maybe he was putting in some extra effort for her. A warmth flamed in her cheeks at the thought. At last, he appeared, hands thrust into his jean pockets as he sauntered out.

"Hi, you played really well tonight," she said, trying to act casual.

"Thanks." He looked over her head to where some cheerleaders had gathered. "Guys"—he nodded at Bennett and Colt—"I'll catch up with you at the party." He took a step toward the uniformed girls.

"Um, I decided I'm going to the party." Misty wasn't sure what was happening, a sick feeling settling in her belly.

"Maybe I'll see you there," he answered distractedly, his attention still focused on the cheerleaders.

"Oh." She swallowed, unsure how to proceed. "I thought I was going with you."

He stopped and swiveled back. "I'm sorry. I think you're really cool and all, but you're not really my"—he cleared his throat—"type."

Misty wanted the ground to open up and swallow her. "Type?" she echoed, dimly aware that her friends had moved away to give her privacy in this mortifying moment.

"Yeah, you know, you're into computers and band, which is cool." He scuffed his boot in the dirt. "But I'm more into sports and rodeo. Bethany"—he pointed at the blonde cheerleader in the distance—"she's been a junior rodeo queen."

"Of course." Misty was frankly amazed that she could even speak over the shattering of her teenage heart.

"I'm sorry if I gave you the wrong idea. I like you, but in a friend kinda way."

"Not in a Bethany-rodeo-queen kinda way."

"No." Logan looked uncomfortably about, clearly wanting to do anything other than have this conversation with her.

"Well, I guess you're right about me not being your type then." She smiled sweetly at him, relief breaking out on his handsome face. "Because I'm nothing like that blonde bimbo." Spinning on her heel, she ran as fast as her feet could take her away from him, tears streaming down her face. Mute evidence of the pain of her first heartbreak.

"Misty," Evelyn called. "Wait up, I'm not as fast as you."

"Make her stop. I think I'm going to die," gasped Indie, dramatically trying to suck in air.

Misty found herself under the bleachers, trash from the night crunching under her feet like autumn leaves. Her nose was running, and she wanted to wail from the agony of her betrayal. "I want to be alone."

"No, you don't," Indie wheezed, clutching at her side. "What you want is ice cream."

"With chocolate fudge sauce and marshmallows and sprinkles and cream," Evelyn said, draping an arm around her forlorn friend. "Guys are jerks."

"Yep." Misty sniffed. "But I really liked that jerk and I thought he liked me."

"I thought he liked you, too," Evelyn agreed.

"Do you want me to get Colt and Bennett to talk to him? Maybe they could rough him up a bit," Indie offered, a gleam of anticipation in her eyes made all the more ghoulish by the poor lighting.

"No." Misty felt embarrassed and stupid. How could she have gotten it so wrong?

"Well, the offer's there." Indie shrugged. "Anytime you ask"—she snapped her fingers—"and I'll make it happen.

Misty laughed. Her friend was terrible. "They would never do it. Logan's their best friend."

"You underestimate my power." Indie took on a super-hero pose, hands on her hips.

"Speaking of power, the ice cream sounded awfully good," Evelyn said.

"Aren't you guys going to the party at the lake?" Misty wiped at her nose.

Evelyn shrugged. "No one will miss me if I don't go."

"I'm sure Bennett will be just fine without me. He knows what would happen if I find out he's been talking to pretty girls." Indie was fierce.

"Then I think I might like that ice cream after all." Misty's friends linked arms with her and walked out from under the bleacher. As they emerged into the artificial light, she made a vow to herself. Never again would she let Logan Erikson make a fool of her.

CHAPTER 1

"If you can make sure we have the latest patches for that software before Tuesday, that would be great." Misty swiveled her chair slightly, turning her gaze to the suavely dressed man beside her. "William, is there anything else you want to add?" She left the question hanging.

Her business partner pursed his soft lips in thought. *I swear the man uses more lip balm than I do.* "No, I think you've covered it all for the moment."

Dana, Misty's PA, discreetly entered the room, dipping her perfectly coiffured head down to her boss's ear. "Your driver is ready to take you to the airport."

Misty nodded her wordless thanks. "Folks, if no one has anything else they want to add, I'm happy to end this meeting."

"You would." William looked up from the manicured nail he'd been inspecting. "Off to play in the dirt again."

"I'd hardly say going to a billionaire's ranch is playing in the dirt," she retorted, gathering her devices from the table.

"Anyway, I mainly stay in the house with Evelyn and the baby."

"Well, don't come back bringing any of that farmyard smell with you." William wrinkled his nose up in mock protest.

"You wouldn't be able to smell it over your own cologne," Misty tartly replied. She loved her business partner, but he could be such a prima donna sometimes, and yet the ladies seemed to eat it up. Each to their own, she guessed, but she liked her men to be real men with calloused hands and five o'clock stubble. *Like Logan,* an irritating voice in her mind whispered.

Shoving her chair in place a little harder than warranted, she spun on her Louboutin's and marched across the polished ebony floor to the door. Misty rather enjoyed the way the silk lining of her skirt slid against her skin as each stride sent a loud *click clack* through the respectfully quiet room. Wealth had its privileges, so did power. And she had both in spades.

"Dana," Misty said, not surprised to have her PA materialize at her side. "Can you please make sure that I'm not disturbed this weekend? Anything urgent can be forwarded to William." She laughed at the droll expression on the other woman's face. Dana had discovered the rare combination of plastic surgery and still remaining fairly natural in a much better-looking version of herself.

"I expect an enormous bonus this year for all the complaining I'll have to put up with," Dana deadpanned. "Now, the plane is stocked with your favorite beverages and I've also arranged a salad from the restaurant you like waiting for your pleasure once you're in the air. Is there anything else you need me to organize?"

"No, I think that's everything."

"Excellent. Then have a safe flight, and I'll see you on

Monday morning." Dana pushed the elevator button for her boss and stepped to one side.

"Thank you, I'll see you in a few days' time."

The elevator doors opened, and Misty stepped inside, praying they would close before someone could find her and delay her with last minute issues. It was with a sense of relief that she felt the familiar plummeting sensation of descent. A few quick minutes after that, she was settled in her town car and being driven away. Misty watched as the cityscape rose up around her, the skyscrapers clawing at the heavens, filled with thousands of people toiling away at their tasks. *Well, not all of them,* she corrected herself. *Some were filled with million-aires and fewer still with billionaires, slaves to their wealth and status.*

She knew how that felt. It was why it was so important to her to make sure she headed back to Colt's family ranch. Her best friend, Evelyn, was waiting for her there, ready to cele-brate Hope's first birthday. Misty hadn't been there since Christmas, and she wasn't going to miss this event for the world. Even if it meant having to see Logan Erikson.

The sharp ring of her phone thankfully prevented her from dwelling too long on that particular cowboy. "Chora, I'm just about to head to the ranch. Did Dana send through the current schedule for this year's gala?"

"She did," the animal charity campaigner replied, a happy energy in her voice.

Misty marveled at how she always managed to have such an upbeat vibe. She'd read some of the stories on her charity website and was pretty sure they weren't the worst of them. And yet Chora remained a glass-half-full kind of gal.

"As usual, it looks like you have everything under control," Chora continued. "I'll start getting this year's star adoption stories together and should have them to you by the end of the month."

"That will be great. I'm about to get on the plane, but I'll touch base with you in a week's time and go over it all in more detail."

"Sure thing, Misty. Say hi to Evelyn and give Hope a kiss for me."

The town car pulled to a smooth halt on the tarmac, a sense of deep satisfaction filling Misty all the way down to her toes. Sitting proudly on the black surface was her gleaming, rose-gold colored pride and joy—her plane. And not just any cheap plane, thank you very much, but a flying statement that Misty Monroe was a success. As far as she was concerned, that alone was more than worth the one hundred million dollars it had cost her. Smiling up at her driver as he opened her door, she accepted his hand and stepped out, her eyes shielded by her oversized sunglasses. Knowing her monogramed leather luggage would be discreetly loaded, she made her way on red-soled pumps toward the waiting hostess. Yes, Misty Monroe had made it, indeed.

THE ENGINE SPLUTTERED before roaring to life, and Logan pumped the accelerator a few times just to be on the safe side. You never did know with the old girl. She could be temperamental at times. He looked up in the rearview mirror, catching sight of remnants of the grease paint he'd failed to remove properly, his bloodshot, tired eyes staring back at him. He had four hours in which to do a six-hour drive, and a betting man wouldn't favor the odds, but that had never stopped Logan before.

Loaded up with a passenger seat piled high with candy and chips and a six pack of energy drinks, he'd make it. Heck, the challenge of it all got the blood flowing. He was the most in-demand Rodeo Protection Athlete in the country and he'd never yet missed a rodeo he was booked in for. He was a professional, after all, and he never let his fans down, even if the siren call of sleep whispered in his ear. It was the price to pay for his fame. One more rodeo, and then he had a party for a very special young lady to get to.

Yep, Logan Erikson had made it, indeed.

CHAPTER 2

*H*er silk pajamas glided across her skin as Misty stretched, refreshed from a good night's sleep. She'd spent so much time at Colt's family ranch over the years that this room had unofficially become hers. Languidly, she lifted her eye mask. There was something about the fresh air that always made her sleep like a baby.

Speaking of baby, today Hope was turning one. Misty couldn't believe it. Memories wormed their way into her mind. This time last year, Indie, Hope's mother, had still been alive. She closed her eyes against the bittersweet torment. It felt like a lifetime since she'd last spoken to her best friend. Gosh, she missed her. Shaking her head to prevent herself from going down that track and glancing at her watch, she pushed back the covers and headed to the shower. There was a birthday girl waiting for her downstairs. Turning the hot water on, she watched the glass shower screen fog up before judging it was perfect for her to step under. As the water cascaded over her body, she closed her eyes in bliss, letting everything leave her mind except for the sensation against her skin.

After a few minutes of relative contentment, Misty reluctantly stepped out and wrapped a heated fluffy towel around her, grabbing another to begin toweling her hair dry. She thoughtfully opened the closet in which the housekeeper, Trixie, had hung her clothes the previous evening. Time to get presentable and go see the birthday girl. Gathering up her packages, she headed to the kitchen.

Buttery goodness assailed her nose, followed by coffee, and there was definitely bacon involved. With her mouth watering, Misty hastened to discover the source for herself. Trixie was ladling scrambled eggs into a dish in preparation for it to join the food already on the table. A mountain of bacon, croissants, biscuits and gravy were already under attack from Colt. Evelyn was blowing on a piece of crispy piggy goodness for Hope, who was already waving her chubby hands about, trying to climb out of her highchair to get to it.

Misty smiled. Now that was a girl after her own heart. "Morning, everyone, and happy birthday, gorgeous girl." She gave Hope a quick kiss, careful not to get between her and the object of her attention. Misty placed her present down.

"Morning, Misty. Did you sleep well?" Evelyn asked, smiling indulgently as Hope finally secured her treasure and began to gnaw on it ravenously.

"I did, as usual." Misty took a plate and began to load it up. "Isn't Mama Evelyn feeding you, you poor child?" she said in mock sympathy to the toddler. "Now, I know that nothing is going to be as good as that bacon you have in your hands, but when we're finished, we can open your present." She broke off a piece of flaky pastry and popped it in her mouth, closing her eyes to better savor it. "Oh my, Trixie, your food is always fabulous, but this is next level. If you ever get sick of putting up with this lot, I'll employ you in a hot minute."

The housekeeper beamed at her happily, placing a cup of coffee in front of her. "It's always good to be appreciated."

"Stop trying to poach Trixie." Colt smiled winsomely up at the housekeeper. "You know we love you," he said, reaching for another helping of eggs. "I mean, what would we do without you?"

"Probably starve. But keep Misty's offer in mind when it's time to give me my bonus." Misty chuckled into her cup at the deadpan look Trixie directed back at the man.

"There's something I want to ask you, and now seems as good a time as any." Evelyn handed Hope another piece of bacon.

"Well?" Misty prompted.

Her friend laughed. "Patience never was one of your strong suits." Evelyn reached over, taking hold of Colt's hand, the diamond on her finger winking in the light. "We've finally decided on a date for the wedding."

"Congratulations, guys." Misty sprung from her chair to give Evelyn a hug and repeated the gesture with Colt. It was about time. They'd only loved each other for, like, forever.

"Thanks." Evelyn brushed back some hair that had been knocked loose from its braid in Misty's enthusiasm. "Which also means there's only one person I would ever consider to be my maid of honor—in fact, you're the only person I'm asking to stand up with me."

Misty swallowed the lump in her throat. Evelyn didn't have to say it. They both keenly felt Indie's absence. "I'd be honored."

"It gets better. I want you to walk down the aisle holding Hope's hand. She's going to be the flower girl."

"She's going to be the cutest little flower girl I ever did see." Misty kissed the toddler on top of her head. "I can't believe you guys finally set a date."

"You and me both," Colt admitted ruefully. "I'm still in

favor of eloping, but Evelyn's dug her heels in over having a real ceremony."

"Yes, a real one. That doesn't mean I want a big one, just something the people I care about can be at. A little intimate gathering here on the ranch." Misty had the feeling that she was missing something from the way Evelyn stressed the word *little*. She was sure her friend would fill in the gaps when they were alone.

"Well, now that's all decided, should we open Auntie Misty's present?" Evelyn picked up the delicately wrapped package.

"I made sure it was wrapped in tissue paper to make it easier for her to open," Misty pointed out.

"Oh, she's good at tearing things apart. She has her mother's ferocity." Colt chuckled as, with perfect timing, Hope set to work, quickly revealing a book inside. He picked it up, looking at it puzzledly. A smile tugged at the corner of his mouth and he looked up at his fiancée. "Can you see what it is?"

"It looks like a coloring book."

"Look closer." He passed it over to her, watching her expectantly.

"Is that us?" Evelyn began to flick through the pages. "There's Indie and Bennett. There's even the Gray's and Freckles. How on earth did you get a coloring book made with Hope's family in it?" Her friend raised awestruck eyes to hers.

"I have a friend who produces those adult coloring books, and it wasn't that hard to arrange for the artists to do images for a book for Hope. All I had to do was supply photos." Misty was feeling rather happy with herself.

"I think I'll put this somewhere safe until Hope can color in between the lines," Evelyn said firmly.

"That's okay, I thought you might say that. I also have a little something else for her." She pushed a little blue box across the table.

Colt picked it up, untying the ribbon to reveal a delicate diamond bracelet with Hope's name engraved on the heart. "Thank you."

"You're welcome." Misty settled back in her chair, pleased that she'd thought to arrange a second gift just in case. "And Evelyn?"

"Yes?"

"I ordered a box of one hundred of those coloring books. Let the kid color however she wants."

Laughter erupted from Evelyn. "All right." She held her hands up in defeat. "I know when I'm beaten." She wrapped an arm around Hope. "And you, miss, are one very lucky girl. Now, give Auntie Misty a thank you kiss."

As a bacon-flavored, slobbery kiss was bestowed on her, Misty couldn't help thinking that she was the lucky one.

"HOLY HECK, is that actually a big top?" Logan lifted his shades to rub his blurry, sleep-deprived eyes. All credit to Evelyn that she'd managed to get Colt to start opening up that wallet of his. It wouldn't have surprised him at all if moths had flown out. On second thought, it might be being wrapped around the finger of a tiny pint-sized dictator. Once Colt had fallen, he'd fallen hard for both of the ladies in his life.

He sandwiched his truck between a van that promised balloon art for the whole family and another that proudly proclaimed the owner as part of the famous flying Lepintz family. Shuddering as he swallowed the last of the warm dregs of energy drink, he quickly found a can of deodorant on the floor of his truck and liberally applied it. Luck was on his side when he found a forgotten stick of gum wedged in the seat.

"Fresh as a daisy," he muttered as he pushed the groaning car door open.

The field beside Colt's mansion was now dominated by the big top. Logan could only imagine what his friend's opinionated horse, Big Wheels, had to make of the brightly colored monstrosity in his domain. Dodging past jugglers and acrobats, he finally found Colt and Evelyn watching as Hope got her face painted. *Just his luck that Misty was there too,* he thought sourly.

"Oh, goody, the clown has arrived," Misty's eyes narrowed as she glared at him. He pulled a face back at her to show just how funny he thought her witty comment was. While he was on it, when was she going to stop looking at him like that? It was enough to make a man irritable. Why couldn't she look at him like most women? That sigh in the there-goes-the-dreamy-Logan-Erikson kind of way he was used to. He'd messed up once—okay, maybe twice—and she insisted on looking at him like she wanted a car to run him over. No, scratch that. A train.

Evelyn helped Hope slide off the face painter's chair, a candy-colored unicorn creation on the birthday girl's face. Logan found himself thinking about how proud Bennett would have been of his little girl. The tiny cherub sure was something. That familiar stab hit him in the gut—the realization that his best friend wasn't there and never would be. Closing his eyes against the pain, he suddenly felt old. Old and tired.

He opened them to see Misty staring at him, her dark eyes assessing. She'd always had that manner about her, though she'd tempered it beneath a shyer exterior—one she'd long since shed. Her wealth of chocolate hair was pulled severely from her face, not a single strand daring to escape. Personally, Logan thought it made her look harder. Knowing it would get on her goat, he couldn't resist winking at her. The way she lifted that determined little chin of hers made the corners of his mouth twitch.

"Something you want to say, Logan?' she challenged.

"Nope, just got something in my eye." He made a show of wiping his face. "All gone now."

"And that's how you solve problems, isn't it? Just make it go away. Or better still, you just leave." The accusing tone of her voice made him wince. *Yep, she wasn't going to forget anytime soon.* From the corner of his eye, he saw Colt and Evelyn exchange a glance.

"All right, kids, time for everyone to simmer down a little." Colt stepped between them as Evelyn took Misty by the arm. "Logan, you want to come look at my cars? I just got the Bugatti back from getting serviced. I reckon it's due for a drive, somewhere I can really open the throttle on it."

Logan was amused to discover that Colt had already maneuvered him several steps away from the beautiful source of his irritation. "Are you going to let me drive it this time?"

"Not on your life. If something happened to it, I'd have to spend my time looking at you the way Misty does." Colt chuckled. "Are you ever going to tell me what happened to make her so mad at you?"

"Nothing happened. I mean, heck, it wasn't that big of a deal." Logan rubbed at his jaw.

He immediately regretted his admission as Colt's face lit with curiosity. "So something *did* happen." Logan glumly knew it was only a matter of time before that particular juicy morsel made its way back to Evelyn and, by default, Misty. "Look, it was nothing. At least not until Misty had to go and turn it into one."

His friend's face grew crafty. "Maybe if you tell me what it is, then I can tell you if Misty's making a mountain out of a molehill. I'm your friend. Let me help."

There was no way Logan was ever going to tell Colt about the time he'd managed to get Misty alone in the hayloft only to fall off the ladder trying to sneak away later on. Or the time he'd set up the mistletoe just so he'd have an excuse to kiss her. Nope, there was no way. He was just about to tell Colt exactly where he could put his generous offer when Evelyn called for everyone to gather around. He'd never been so relieved in his whole life to sing happy birthday and watch a kid blow a candle out on a cake.

And what a cake it was—four tiers high. The bottom tier had what looked to be a grand circus parade going around it, women balancing on horseback, bears on tiny tricycles, lions, camels and elephants. The next had juggling clowns and leaping acrobats, and the second last tier had the trapeze artists flying gracefully across a floodlit background. The pièce de résistance was the big, proud top layer, its red and white sides holding a banner high with the number one on it. Yep, it sure was something.

Evelyn clapped her hands together once more as Colt gestured for silence. "Thank you everyone for coming today," he began, his arm around Evelyn as she held Hope on her hip. "Hope is one lucky gal to have so many people who love her, especially her poppy and gammie." He nodded toward her grandparents who beamed back. For a moment, Colt paused and looked heavenward, Hope's parents clearly on his mind. Logan could see him swallow painfully, emotion getting the better of him. Colt leaned over and kissed the squirming toddler. "Happy Birthday, Hope." A cheer went up.

As was often the case, a lull fell over the gathered audience, muttering to each other, unsure what to do next. Logan saw his opportunity. "Happy Birthday to you," he began to sing, and before long the refrain was picked up. Colt smiled gratefully at him.

After the mandatory pictures were taken with family in front of the cake, Trixie cut great slabs to hand out. Logan was eyeing the chocolatey goodness when Colt appeared and handed him a plate. "Thanks, I wasn't sure if there was going to be enough for everyone."

Colt laughed. "I think I'm going to be eating that cake for the next month. Misty had it flown in especially from Las Vegas on her plane from a Mary? Maria? Marie?" He shook his head, giving up."

"Of course Misty did," Logan said sourly.

She just had to make sure everyone knew she had her own plane. Heck, Colt's just as rich and he doesn't feel the need to have one. Sure, Bryce—Colt's business partner who was also a billionaire and here with his wife—had one, but you never heard him mention it. Logan shoveled a piece of cake in his mouth to stop him from saying anything nasty. An explosion of caramel popcorn robbed him of all reason. Eyes opened wide, he stared at Colt.

"You were saying?" prompted Colt.

"Okay, so maybe this time it was worth having a private plane." He grinned, pulling a face at Hope to get her to giggle as Evelyn walked about and wrapped an arm around his friend. "How good is the cake?" she asked.

"It's okay," Logan deadpanned, laughing at her outraged expression. "Okay, it's almost as good as s—" He broke off, looking at the giggling little girl guiltily. "Um, it's really good."

Colt kissed the top of Evelyn's head. "You did good, babe." The way they looked at each other—they looked happy and in love. And they deserved to be. Logan always had kind of known that Colt was sweet on her, and the way she gazed up at him … well, Colt was one lucky man. Kind of left a man hunkering for that sort of luck himself.

igh in her Manhattan Penthouse, Misty felt like a princess in her fairytale castle amongst the clouds. Tonight the weather had turned ugly, the skyline blurred into abstract art. Tomorrow when it cleared, she'd be able to see the Hudson River and Central Park from her rooftop terrace, but for now, she was snug inside. She wandered out of her climate-controlled shoe and handbag closet, having slipped off her shoes as she'd listened to her mother make small talk about the weather and her latest hobbies. Misty knew the real reason she'd called would be revealed in due time. Frankly, she just wished her mom would hurry up and get to the point. She paused to activate the lock to her closet with her thumb print. With the contents in that room worth more than most people's houses, it was prudent to keep it secure.

"—and then I told Agnes that if she didn't want to share her recipe, then neither would I."

"I guess that's fair." Misty stepped into her clothing closet, looking at the carefully catalogued contents organized by season, dress code, fabric and color. After a long day at work, all she wanted to do was grab some fresh pajamas off the shelf and soak in a steaming, fragrant bath. Snatching some, she headed back into her master bedroom. "So, Mom, I really should be going. It was great to catch up."

"Brandon's getting out of jail soon."

Misty's gaze jagged to the floor-to-ceiling windows framing the room as she sunk onto her bed at the mention of her brother. "When?"

"The end of the month. Your father and I were thinking that you could lend him some money, help him get back on his feet." The wheedling tone in her mother's voice set Misty's teeth on edge. How she wished the night outside was clear and she could lose herself in the bright lights, but the whimsy of the clouds had turned dark like her mood.

"I don't think so. He's taken more than enough from me. The money I gave and the money he stole from me and you and Dad all ended up in his arm. Never again."

"He's changed."

"I'll believe that when I see it." Misty rubbed the bridge of her nose, feeling the beginning of a tension headache. "Where's he staying? He'll have parole again, I imagine."

"Well, we thought…"

"That he could stay with you in the condo I pay for?" Bitterness that she would still have to pay for him—even if indirectly—made her want to slam the phone down. But that level of petulance was far beneath her now. "Is there anything else you called to talk about? I'm almost at my peak capacity for good news from you right now."

"Well, we're having some difficulty with the AC. Can you arrange someone to fix it? It gets hot here in Florida without one."

"I'll get Dana to arrange something when I get into the office tomorrow." *I'm going to need to take a bottle of wine to the bath with me to recover from this phone call.*

"And could you put a little extra into our account this month? Your father wants to go on a fishing charter."

"And you can't pay for it out of the thirty thousand dollars a month allowance I give you?" *At what point did I become an ATM for my parents?*

"Well, that money goes on other expenses."

Misty's brows shot up. "I purchased both cars you drive, I paid for the condo and all the utilities. What the heck other expenses do you have that costs more than thirty thousand dollars in one month?"

"That's none of your business, young lady. Anyway, it's not like you can't afford it."

"You're right. It's not like I can't afford it, no thanks to you and Daddy. I paid my own way through college when you and Daddy were too busy with Brandon. I'm the one who worked three jobs to raise the capital for my company, and I'm the one who gets up at four-thirty in the morning to start my day. I'd say I earned every dang dollar I have."

"Well, I never. You remember who you're talking to, Misty Monroe," her mother spluttered. She could just imagine her clutching at her chest like she was about to have a heart attack.

"Yeah, I know exactly who I'm talking to. Goodnight, Mom." The satisfaction of hanging up on her mother was short-lived. She knew that, tomorrow, she'd transfer that money. A child's guilt and all that.

Deciding she was too keyed up, she headed to the kitchen and opened the refrigerator. Thank goodness for Jeremy. Her chef had stocked it up with carefully packaged meals for her. A little post-it note was stuck to the one nearest her. Curiously, she pulled it off to read.

Misty, my darling, make sure you give your body the fuel it needs to make magic happen. But if that's not enough, I've made five different desserts to get you through the week.

J

Bless him. What would she do without him? Probably have to see her personal trainer a lot less. Snagging a container of tiramisu before a quick detour to the wine cellar to liberate a bottle of Chateau d'Yquem, she headed to the bathroom. Nothing was going to get her night back on track like dessert, wine, and a long hot soak in a tub. As she settled in, she made a mental note to get Dana to book her in for a facial and massage. Heck, it would mean working till midnight even with having scheduled her PT session for four-thirty in the morning, but it would be worth it.

As she sipped on her wine and savored spoonfuls of dessert in the steamy relaxation of the tub, she marveled at how far she'd come. A sneaking suspicion that she hadn't come far enough intruded into her feelings of contentment. Taking another sip, she determinedly buried the thoughts. She was living her best life, and that's all there was to it.

THE PROTECTION VEST had seen better days, but then again, so had he. Logan ran his fingers over the long rend that ran from one side to the other, the only thing that had stopped old Angry Bird from goring his innards out at that rodeo up at Cheyenne. Sliding it into place and fastening it securely, he reached for his brightly colored sponsor shirt and baggy bull fighting skirt, colorful scarves dangling. Holding on to the side of his pickup for balance, he wondered how many miles he'd done since he'd saved up every penny he had to buy it. Maybe it was time to trade the old girl in. Nah, that beaten-up old truck had been the longest relationship he'd ever had. He'd miss her if she wasn't there.

Pulling the wing mirror to him, he began to apply the face paint. Tonight he'd been hired to be the barrel man. As he smeared the thick white paint on, he saw the face the crowds wanted to see appear—the clown. Not Logan. As all traces of him disappeared, he knew tonight would be just like every night. The roar of the crowd filling his ears as he danced with the enraged bovines, making cracks with the commentator and acting the fool. No one would remember his daringness as he protected the fallen cowboys. Only the clown.

And then later, another nameless girl would giggle that she couldn't wait to tell all her friends that she'd hooked up with the clown. It was a life he'd thrived on, but now it had lost its gloss and turned brassy. Giving a final swipe at his face, he pulled a tattered hat firmly down over his forehead. Showtime.

CHAPTER 4

The latest figures for the quarter flashed across Misty's computer screen. Dipping a carrot stick in some hummus, she munched her lunch as she read the spreadsheet. Expanding into smart devices was proving to be as lucrative as she'd hoped.

"My, you're positively glowing. I can't imagine it's the vegetable you're eating that's causing such a reaction." William sauntered into Misty's office, immaculate as usual in a navy tailored suit. "Poor Jeremy must have felt slighted to find out that was what he would be preparing you for lunch."

Misty took a satisfying crunch out of the maligned orange stick. "Well, after all the desserts he's been stuffing me full with, it was either this or start tripling my PT sessions. Honestly, I don't think my glutes could've taken it." She smiled at her partner. "And thank you. I tried the new light treatment when I had my facial."

"I must try it when I'm there next." He unbuttoned his jacket as he took a seat opposite her. "I got your email to come see you."

"It wasn't urgent, but I appreciate you coming so promptly." A low thrill began to build inside her. There was nothing like the adrenaline of pitching an idea. In some ways, it was harder to impress William—he'd already heard it all from her. "What do you know about lotus silk?"

"I know all about silk-silk, but I don't think I've ever heard about lotus silk." His perfectly sculpted brow furrowed. "Is it a new brand?"

"No, it's a different material. It's harvested from the stem of a lotus flower, which currently is a waste product. It takes twenty-five women to harvest enough thread for one weaver to work with, and that weaver can only make one meter of fabric a day."

"Sounds like it's expensive." A gleam of calculating interest appeared in William's eyes.

Misty relaxed. She knew she had him on the hook. "It is."

"What does it look like?"

"Like a blend of linen and silk. It's wrinkle resistant, breathable, soft, light. Actually, it's the first natural microfiber. In fact, it's probably the most ecofriendly product in the world as no pollution-making energy is used throughout the entirety of the production process."

William steepled his fingers under his chin, considering the idea. "Everyone wants ecofriendly credentials these days. Is this something you're looking at the company investing in?"

"In an indirect way. I've been approached about providing the funds for a charity that helps women in Third World countries get set up in business, and something that's been flagged a few times is lotus silk. What I'm wondering is if we can create a market for it." Misty looked at William, seeing him turn the possibilities over in his astute mind. "I know you love your fashion as much as I do. Would you care to come onboard, see if we can have lotus silk become the hot new fashion textile?"

William struck a nonchalant pose, as effortlessly chic as a runway model. "Of course, darling. I can't let you have all the fun."

It was hard to remember how awkward they'd both been in college. They'd become friends in their first class and stuck together through thick and thin. Gosh, so much had changed for them in the past decade.

"Now that's been decided, on to important matters." William fixed her with an intense gaze. "Do you have any requests for what suit I should pack for the wedding?"

She considered toying with him. William had the most exquisite dress sense of anyone she knew. "No matter what ends up in your carry on, you're going to look extremely handsome." Misty smiled at him. "Just don't look too gorgeous. I don't want you upstaging the groom."

William's eyes twinkled at the prospect. "I wouldn't dare. Now I need to go through my suit inventory. Only the best if I'm going to be the date of the most beautiful woman—after the bride, that is." And with a naughty little wink, he left her alone to her figures. Thank goodness William had agreed to be her plus one. He was just what she needed to get through this wedding and its best man.

Growing up, Logan and his sister had spent a few years living in a trailer till his parents had managed to scrape enough money together to buy their ranch. It sure as heck didn't look anything like the one Colt had hired for the night before his wedding. To be fair, this wasn't some pokey double wide—it was a fully decked out RV.

"I didn't know you could get ones that popped out and up." Mr Gray cradled a tumbler of whiskey to his chest, peering at the engineering marvel that enveloped him.

"Bryce told me about the trailers they had set up for that movie they shot for Luciano Navarro—you know the one that came out a few summers ago about the bull rider and the barrel racer?" Colt topped up Logan's glass as he spoke. "Anyway, when Evelyn made it very clear that I wasn't going to be spending the night before our wedding in the house, I thought, what better way to spend it than living the best bachelor life possible in an RV?"

"I'm not complaining, but surely your house is big enough that we could've just taken up one end of it. They wouldn't even know we were there." Logan enjoyed the way the aged whiskey slid smoothly down his throat. He leaned back in the black leather sofa and crossed his legs comfortably in front of him. Heck, all he was missing was the cigar.

"Evelyn said it was bad luck to spend the night before the wedding under the same roof. Or get ready together, for that matter. With how the Montgomery's luck has been, we decided not to risk it."

Logan nodded in understanding, thinking of those who were gone but dearly missed on occasions like this. Privately he thought it was best not to chance running into Misty either. Visions of her in a silken robe as her and Evelyn had pillow fights bouncing on the bed momentarily distracted him. The sound of Mr Gray clearing his throat snapped him out of that particularly enjoyable fantasy.

"Thank you for inviting me. I know you didn't have to," the old man said, not quite meeting Colt's eye. It almost surprised Logan that Bennett had been so openly caring and happy when you considered what his dad was like.

"Mr Gray, you're Hope's grandfather and, more than that, I consider you my family too. It's nice to have a father figure here tonight."

"Any advice for the young man before he embarks on married life?" Logan couldn't resist teasing, laughing when the old man turned beet red. "How about the wedding night?"

"I don't know about all that," Mr Gray blustered.

"Mrs Gray always seems like a satisfied woman," Logan prompted.

"Logan Erikson, behave yourself. You ain't too old for a good thrashing," the old man threatened, setting his glass down on the table. Logan held his hands up in surrender. "Now, there's something I want to give you, Colt." Mr Gray held his hand open to reveal an engraved silver pocket watch. "I gave this to Bennet when he turned eighteen. It used to be his grandfather's. He used to tell me he planned on wearing it when he married Indie. Now I want you to have it," he finished gruffly.

Logan looked into his drink, willing himself invisible in this private moment between a father still mourning his son and the man he now considered family. Swallowing his own emotions down, he looked up. Usually he wasn't into airy-fairy type stuff, but for a moment, he swore he saw Bennett standing behind his father, his hand resting over the watch as if to bless it, his trademark grin beaming at Colt. Logan blinked, disappointment flashing bright when Bennett was no longer there, followed by a sense of peace. Not that he'd ever tell anyone what he thought he'd just seen. This one was strictly between him and Bennett.

"Now, Mrs Gray has given me strict instructions not to stay out all night with you young bucks. She wants me to look presentable tomorrow. And you know what they say— or at least you soon will —happy wife, happy life." The old man gave a wink at them both and then left them to it.

Logan scratched at a mark on his jeans with his nail. "You heard the old man. Happy wife, happy life. You sure you aren't going to miss bachelor life? It sounds like it's more fun not being bossed around all the time by Evelyn—or Hope for that matter."

The huge grin that broke out over Colt's face was answer enough. "No way. I've lived that life hard, man, and there's nothing like knowing that Evelyn and Hope are who I'm coming home to." He gave a rueful shrug. "Even if it is just to be bossed around by them. Anyway, they already do. Something I've discovered is that women only seem to do that to men they care about. You should try it sometime."

Logan almost choked on the whiskey he'd just attempted to swallow. Colt helpfully thumped him on the back, clearly enjoying it a little too much given the vigor of which he set to the task. "Not likely. I'm not that kind of man." He shuddered in horror. "I'm not that kind of man," he repeated, unsure if it was for Colt's or his benefit.

"I think every man is deep down." Colt grinned as if he knew a secret Logan didn't. "With the right woman."

ears began to fill Evelyn's large dark eyes as she sat, ready for the makeup artist to set to work, the phone held to her ear with a trembling hand. "Okay, but Mom, I really need you and Dad here today."

Misty, having fully embraced her maid of honor duties, held out her hand for the phone. She needed her bride to be calm and happy, not blotchy-faced and red-eyed. Whatever the problem was, it was up to her to solve. "Hello, Mrs Hart, it's Misty. What happened?"

A long-winded ramble spilled through the earpiece of missing ties and taxis not showing up. At one point, there was a theory that the dog had eaten a passport. Misty blinked. *Okay then...* "So where are you now? Still in New Zealand?"

"No, we made it to Las Angeles, but we missed our connecting flight to Texas and they're not sure when we can get on another one. Right now, it doesn't look like we'll get there in time for the wedding," she wailed down the phone, clearly loud enough for Evelyn to hear. Evelyn began to tear up again.

Misty handed her friend a tissue. "Mrs Hart, here's what's going to happen." She was all business. "You need to get yourself, Mr Hart and your luggage over to the private terminal. In fact, forget that, go to the members' lounge. I'll have someone meet you there. Don't worry, I'll have you both here in time to see Evelyn finally catch Colt." She looked impishly up at her friend. "I mean, get married." Her job done, she handed the phone back to Evelyn and pulled her own one out. A few quick calls and her private plane was on its way to collect some very frazzled parents of the bride.

"Thanks, Misty." Evelyn looked at her gratefully before the makeup artist requested she close her eyes.

"Only your parents would get all the way from New Zealand after crossing floods and saving passports from wild dogs to not be able to get a connecting flight from LA to Houston."

Evelyn giggled, causing the makeup artist to frown in annoyance. "New Zealand isn't that big. I mean, I think they live, like, forty minutes away from the international airport on the South Island."

"Honestly, that doesn't surprise me." She glanced down at her watch. "I'm just going to duck out for a few minutes. It doesn't look like you're going anywhere, anyway."

"Misty, it's all under control."

"I know, but I just want to check for myself." Escaping out the door before Evelyn could protest more, Misty quickly made her way down the hall before turning right through the library and opening a pair of French doors to reveal the marvel that met her seeking eyes. The glistening white marquee glowed under the golden light of the early morning sun, large and imperial among a sea of emerald green grass, the trees provided a textured backdrop to its purity. Misty sniffed in approval. It would be more than sufficient to hold all of Colt and Evelyn's guests for the reception.

"I see I'm not the only one who didn't entirely trust the wedding planner, no matter her credentials." Trixie handed a steaming cup of coffee to her.

The translucent wisps of vapor somehow seemed tangible and ethereal at the same time. Real in that moment before disappearing. Misty smiled at the whimsy. "Yeah, I just want everything to be perfect for them. They deserve it."

The housekeeper smiled over the rim of her own mug. "I agree. It's why I thought I'd quickly take the chance to snoop on the progress while Hope was still asleep. How's the bride?"

"She picked at the breakfast you left us and now she's in the hands of the makeup artist and hairstylist. I should probably get back to her."

"Have you seen the porch yet?"

Misty shook her head. The porch was where Colt and Evelyn had decided to hold their ceremony, both saying it felt like home to them and that it summed up how it felt when they finally allowed themselves to be a family. "No, I haven't."

With an excited gleam in her eyes, Trixie quickly headed to the front of the house. Misty stopped dead, blinking back tears at the sight. Floral garlands of white roses, jasmine and Texas bluebells were wrapped around the supporting posts, a soft white carpet flowing down the stairs and up the aisle, white chairs lining it, to another floral arch that Evelyn would appear under when the guests would first see her. But it was the porch swing that held her gaze. A fantastically wrought glass floral garland of sunflower yellow and cobalt blue lay in the center, a large white pillar candle rising out of it with two wicks.

She held a hand to her mouth. "She made sure they'd be here, like we always said we would when we got married." Indie would have been swirling around, singing and making them both laugh—the lightness to her seriousness. Misty reached out and gave Trixie's hand a squeeze. "Thank you for showing this to me so I wouldn't see it for the first time with one hundred wedding guests watching me sob like a little baby." The housekeeper smiled in gentle understanding, and Misty gave a final determined sniff. "I better get back and make sure Evelyn is so beautiful that Colt plumb forgets his vows."

And Good Lord, but she was beautiful, her face glowing as Misty helped lower her veil in place. The strapless gown was covered in hand-beaded crystals that shimmered and shone with every minute movement. Misty's own pale pink gown that had a similar treatment, along with Hope's confectionery of tulle, was a perfect match, putting her in mind of diamonds. She hugged Evelyn close, careful not to muss her perfection.

"I swore I wouldn't cry, but you look like a fairy princess. All crystal."

"You look amazing, too," Evelyn said, blinking rapidly.

Misty smoothed down the tight-fitting gown. "Not too amazing, I hope."

"Well, let's just say that if I didn't love you so much, I'd be jealous." Evelyn picked up an intricate glass basket, the detail pure perfection, and handed it to Misty. "Can you please put some rose petals from that bag over there in this? I think we're almost ready to go." She looked sadly down. "I really hoped Mom and Dad would get here in—"

"We made it!" The door slammed against the wall as Mrs and Mr Hart made their dramatic entrance, hair messed, clothing askew, but very much having made it in time.

"Mom! Dad!" Evelyn shrieked, causing Hope to cover her ears with her hands. "I'd given up."

"Never give up on a Hart." Her father wagged his finger

sternly. "It might not be pretty, but we always get there in the end."

If someone sends a private plane for you, Misty couldn't help thinking.

"Our baby looks beautiful," Mrs Hart said tearily to her husband.

"She sure does."

"Mr and Mrs Hart, the wedding is about to start, if you go and find your seat, it will give us enough time to get Evelyn where she needs to be for the ceremony." Misty knew there were going to be major delays if she didn't interrupt. The Harts didn't tend to have the firmest grasp on things like schedules, time, organization…

More kisses and hugs and then Misty safely got them out of the room. Evelyn bit down on her lip as if to stifle laughter. "I do love them, I really do, but they always have the worst timing. Thanks for not letting it get out of hand. I'll have plenty of time to catch up with them after the wedding."

Misty shrugged matter-of-factly. "It's all part of the job." She scooped up the petals and placed them in Hope's glass basket, safely setting it down on the table as she fetched the bridal bouquet and handed it to Evelyn. "Another part of my job is making sure the beautiful, blushing bride actually makes it to the aisle." She paused, her gaze sweeping over her best friend. "You look beautiful, and I can't believe that today Evelyn Hart is marrying Colt Montgomery. Sixteen-year-old you must be beside yourself. You know his eyes are totally going to bug out when he sees how beautiful little Evelyn looks as his bride."

A becoming blush swept her cheeks. "Thanks, Misty. It doesn't really seem real, but at the same time, it feels so right." Evelyn gathered up her skirts in one hand. "Now, help me get to the top of that aisle without falling over."

Misty hooked an arm through the flower girl's basket

and, with the same hand, reached out to her friend, the other to take Hope's. "Ladies, are we ready?"

"Yes." The nervous lick Evelyn gave her red lips might have slightly ruined the confident tone she was going for.

"Well, let's go get you hitched."

LOGAN WAS NO MORE than passing acquaintances with most of the guests who had gathered, but there were some familiar faces as he scanned the crowd from his place beside Colt. The Gray's were obviously front and center, and Evelyn's parents had just bustled in, breathless, in the eleventh hour—like usual. It wouldn't have surprised him if they'd somehow managed to mess up arrangements to come to their own daughter's wedding, it's the kind of thing they were renowned for. Jackson, a bull rider that he knew, was there with his new wife, as well as a couple they appeared to know well. He recognized Bryce and Savannah, as well as Trixie and Nurse Inger. And Logan's sister, Shelby, was seated beside an immaculately dressed man who looked vaguely familiar.

"Do you think she'll be here soon?" Colt asked for the hundredth time, eagerly looking to the top of the aisle like it would magically make his bride appear, his smile equal parts nerves and excitement.

"She'll be here when she's meant to be. Do you honestly think Misty would let her be late?" That woman was wound so tight she was practically her own watch.

Colt raked slightly trembling hands through his hair. "No, I guess you're right."

No sooner had the words left his mouth when the string orchestra struck up a tune. Framed by the arch, Misty appeared, resplendent in sparkling, dusky pink and holding

Hope's hand in hers, the little girl's eyes huge as everyone turned around to stare. Misty bent down to give the toddler an encouraging kiss, but Hope was frozen to the spot. After the briefest of hesitations, Misty scooped her up and placed her on her hip. Logan had to give it to her. She walked down that aisle like a queen, hands down the most gorgeous thing he'd ever seen. Her hair was in soft dark curls framing her heart-shaped face, and her eyes sparkled with the knowledge of being the center of attention and the certainty of just how fine she looked.

When those liquid eyes met his, it hit him in the chest like a thunderbolt. He watched as her lips parted slightly, and he knew she felt the intensity spring to life between them, too. And then she took her place, hidden from his view, as the music changed and beside him Colt eagerly turned to gaze adoringly at his waiting bride. It was all Logan could do to school his expression to pleasant blandness, unnerved by what had passed between him and Misty.

Logan was still chewing over his discomfort at his extreme reaction later as he watched Misty dance with the gussied-up dandy who had been sitting next to Shelby. Memories flashed through his mind, tormenting him of them—much younger—dancing together, a time when she'd still been untested by life and had been as soft and yielding as silk. Who the heck was that guy to be holding her like that, anyway? Colt hadn't mentioned anything about Misty having a boyfriend. Whispering something into the shmuck's ear, she gracefully made her way to the bar. Logan felt a little thirsty himself.

"I didn't know you like pretty boys," he said, claiming the space beside her.

"At least he's civilized," she retorted, a slight narrowing of her eyes making him grin.

Smugly, he winked at her, enjoying the way her gorgeous

mouth flattened to an uncompromising slash of red. "You didn't have a problem that Christmas when we—"

Misty stiffened as if he'd struck her. "Well, I was mistaken, because what I thought you were offering was very different to your intentions."

Logan didn't like the guilt that followed her words. Gesturing to the bartender, he ordered a shot of tequila, impatiently waiting for her to set it down in front of him. Squeezing the lime into it, he threw down the fiery clear liquid before throwing the salt over his shoulder, anything to get rid of the devil who always seemed to be there when he was around Misty. He rested an elbow on the bar.

"Look, lady, I ain't ever promised you nothing I didn't deliver." Logan pushed himself off the bar without waiting for a reply.

"Like in high school?" She bit back, causing him to pause in his escape. "I remember a lot of promises back then." Her tone was velvet yet edged in steel. Steel that slammed hard into Logan's gut.

"Geeze, Misty, I was seventeen back then. Teenage boys are jerks."

"Yeah, well, so are the men they grow into."

For a moment, words gathered in his mouth before, leaving them unspoken, he stalked away.

How she hated that man! He'd even had the gall to stand there looking handsome as all heck with his pale blue eyes and strong, rugged face, staring at her like she was a piece of chocolate cake he wanted to eat up. Misty had spent most of the reception trying to ignore the fact that he was even still breathing, which had been trying, to say the least, especially when the bridal party photos were being taken. Being all pals, Logan had joked around with Colt, giving Evelyn outrageous compliments and tickling Hope. Misty had satisfied herself with giving him the evil eye. In fact, she would be surprised if her glaring at him didn't appear in one of the final portraits. Darn, but she wanted to wipe that smug smile right off his—

"Can I get you anything, miss?" the bartender asked respectfully.

"Actually, that's a great idea, I'll have a shot of tequila as well." As soon as it was placed in front of her, she picked it up, her hand trembling with anger. He'd always been able to bring out strong emotions in her, despite her best attempts to feel neutral. She licked the inside of her palm, dusting it in salt, before throwing her head back and downing the shot and picking up the lime wedge and sucking on it. The tartness made her lips pucker.

A hand clasped her on the shoulder. "That's the spirit," Shelby said. "We're here to paint the town and the front porch and all that liquor ain't going to drink itself."

"Nothing says have a drink like a wedding," Misty agreed as Shelby settled into the spot that Logan had occupied. His sister shared the same coloring as him, but was a prettier, tomboy version.

"You sure are looking fancy." Shelby eyed her up and down. "You know Mom still asks about you. She says you're the one who got away."

Misty was stunned that she was even still a subject of conversation at the Erikson household. "Yeah, well, you can tell her she's wrong. He's the one who leaves." She couldn't quite hide the bitterness in her voice.

Shelby shrugged as she accepted a drink. "Maybe he figures you're out of his league and that if he doesn't do the leaving, you will. He always has been prickly about rejection. I reckon getting him to admit it would be harder than putting socks on a rooster." She sipped her drink, unaware of the way Misty stared at her in dumbfounded silence. "Anyway, you've got your fancy-pants new boyfriend now."

Misty blinked, uncomfortably aware that she'd lost control of the conversation. "William?"

"If that's his name."

She laughed while briefly wondering if she should play along with it. "He's just my business partner and friend, nothing more."

Shelby looked over her shoulder to where William was now deep in conversation with Bryce and Colt. "What a waste." Misty followed her gaze, but instead found Logan standing with the Gray's. *What a waste, indeed.*

CHAPTER 6

For once Misty didn't saunter down for breakfast feeling well rested. Everyone had celebrated the Montgomery's wedding well into the night and, after quite a few shots of tequila mixed with champagne, she wasn't feeling quite as sprightly as she usually did. Even Trixie seemed a little bleary-eyed when she greeted her with a plate full of food as she pulled up a chair.

"Are the newlyweds still here?" Misty asked quietly. Heck, it was unnerving how quiet the house was.

"You just missed them. I told Colt when he booked their flights that he was living dangerously, booking them for first thing after getting married. But did he listen to me? No. All he said was that he was very keen to start his honeymoon," huffed the housekeeper.

Misty's brows arched skywards. "I can imagine. That man must have one heck of an itch to scratch." She made a show of looking around. "And is Hope still sleeping?" It was going to be good, hanging out on the ranch with Hope and Trixie while her parents were away.

"Yep, she was worn out from her big day yesterday. They both gave her a kiss before they left." Trixie fixed a plate for herself and came to the table. "The little darling looked cute as pie in her big girl dress."

"She sure did." Misty took a forkful of the scrambled eggs, detecting a hint of truffle. Trixie sure did know how to make a first-class breakfast.

"Are the lovebirds still in bed?" The rumble of a low masculine voice turned the eggs to dust. Trust Logan to ruin her appetite.

"You're not much of a best man if you don't even know what time they left for their honeymoon," Misty said tartly, conveniently forgetting she'd done the same.

"I'm amazed you're even awake. Where's lover boy?"

"Still in bed, I assume."

"Not much of a man if you can wear him out so easily."

"At least he's still there in the morning." A tightness began to grip Misty's chest, a wheeze rattling. *Oh no, not now.*

"Sometimes it's better to leave the ladies wanting more." Logan peered intently at her, concern furrowing his brow.

"What would you know about ladies?" The tightness ratcheted up, making it impossible to breathe.

He sprung to his feet, catching her when her knees slowly gave way as she struggled to get air. "Trixie, quick, you need to go get her inhaler. She usually keeps one in her bag." Misty closed her eyes against the world, torturously struggling against the vice in her chest. "Misty, I need you to calm down, imagine it's like a wave. Nice and easy." His voice soothed as he brushed the hair back from her face before loosening it. "Nice and easy." Misty clung to his words like a lifeline.

"I found it." Trixie's worried voice was triumphant as she rushed back to their sides, pressing it into Misty's hands.

Giving it a shake, she held the Ventolin to her lips and inhaled, focusing on her breathing, each rise of her chest slightly higher than the one before. Once she had control again—and that was one of the things she hated the most about her asthma attacks, the complete loss of control over something as fundamental as breathing—she opened her eyes to find Logan's worried face peering into her own, Trixie's peeking over his shoulder.

"I'm okay now."

"Are you sure?" Logan asked, obviously not convinced after what he'd just witnessed.

"Yeah, I think I'll go lie down for a while." Misty let him gently pull her to her feet. As she began to make her way up to her room, it became clear that Logan intended to escort her. "You don't need to walk me to my room."

"I know, but I'd feel better if I did." He glanced sideways at her from the corner of his eyes, his golden eyelashes pale. "Has your asthma gotten worse?"

She awkwardly gathered her robe around herself, conscious of her messy hair tumbling around her shoulders. "A bit. I think it's from all the pollution in the air when I'm in New York. It's not so bad when I go to my house in the Hamptons."

"Of course." Sarcastic undertones laced Logan's voice. "You never wear your hair down anymore." He reached a hand out to tentatively touch her mussed tresses. "It's always pulled back, like you have to have it under control."

Self-consciously, Misty raised a hand to her ruined hairstyle. "I need to look professional. It's important that people take me seriously."

Logan stared at her incredulously. "And you think your hairstyle is going to make people do that? You're kidding, right? It's your presence, the steel in your gaze, that tells people not to mess with you. I reckon most people don't even get to your hair."

"You did."

"That's because I knew you before you could turn a man to stone with a single look. Heck, Misty, I'm sorry. You know, about what happened that time." He cleared his throat, the apology sticking uncomfortably. Misty wondered if he was going to choke on it. "It really was a misunderstanding. And while I'm at it, I might as well clear the slate. I'm sorry about being a jerk in high school, too."

She stared at him, slack-jawed, her hand resting on the doorhandle of her bedroom. "I don't know what to say. Thank you, I guess."

"I'll just enjoy the fact you were speechless for at least a second." Deep grooves appeared on the sides of his mouth as he smiled at her. He really was devastatingly handsome. "Do you still dance?"

Misty blinked at the rapid change in subject. "Not as much as I'd like to," she admitted. "Work pretty much consumes my life." She'd die before she told him she'd never met anyone she liked dancing with as much as him. Under the moonlight, beside the lake like they did that summer… "So, does this mean you aren't going to be such a jerk now?"

"I'll try. It's just that I like Misty. Not Misty Monroe, the billionaire."

The careful truce between them snapped in a heartbeat. "Well, that's going to be a problem since I'm one and the same and I don't intend on changing for your insecure male ego."

"Yeah, well, Misty used to be a sweetheart. Misty the billionaire can be a real b—"

"How dare you," Misty snapped, fighting the urge to slap him across his smug, handsome face.

"I even said I'm sorry and I'm not." Logan leaned in close

until his eyes were level with hers, spitting icy fire at her. "I'm not sorry for what happened at all. In fact, I enjoyed every minute of it. And if you're honest with yourself, so did you." He straightened up. "You're the one who had to go and make it more complicated than it needed to be."

As Logan stalked down the hall, Misty, in a fit of pique, stooped and took her slipper off to hurl at him. The fact he easily dodged it made her give a frustrated shriek. Instead she contented herself with slamming the bedroom door closed behind her. Dramatically, she flopped on the bed and pulled the covers over her head. Logan Erikson could go rot, as far as she was concerned.

WHY DID Misty always have to be so stubborn? Heck, she'd gone and ruined a perfectly good apology with being pigheaded. Logan gunned the engine of his truck, flooring it as he flew away from the house and the annoying woman inside it. For a moment he considered calling Colt, but remembered his best friend was off being a married man. Pursing his lips, he decided he was going to have to go for second best.

Logan found his sister lying underneath an old Trans Am, radio blaring bad eighties music. "Alex the seal," she sang at the top of her lungs as he walked over from his truck.

"You know that's not the lyrics, right?"

Shelby pushed herself out to peer up at him, squinting in the sun. "Of course it is. You can hear them say it clear as day."

He shook his head at her denial. "Why would they be singing about a seal?"

"Because they're cute."

"No, Shelby, it's *our lips are sealed.*"

His sister rubbed at her nose, leaving a trail of grease in its wake. "Are you sure?"

He nodded. "Yeah."

She held her hand out for him to help her up. "Next time it plays, I'll listen real hard and see if you're right. Till then I'm going to remain unconvinced."

Logan smiled at her. His kid sister had never been a pushover. "How's the car coming along?" He gestured to the beat-up old car she'd purchased with just about everything either hanging off or already hitting the dirt.

"I'm waiting on some more parts, but she's going to purr when she's finished." She patted the side of the car. "She's gonna go faster than a prairie fire with a tailwind. Aren't you, my beauty?"

"If anyone's going to make this car into a dream, it's you." She'd always had a talent for seeing beneath the façade of things to the true value underneath.

"Speaking of dreamy, how much of a good match would Billy and Misty be? He's so yummy." She sighed, holding her hands together over her heart.

The last thing Logan wanted to talk about was Misty's new boyfriend. "Isn't his name William?"

"Yeah, but Billy seems like a better fit." It gave Logan a great deal of satisfaction knowing how much the dressed-up peacock would probably hate being called that. Billy it was, then.

Her words sunk in. "Hang on, what do you mean *would be*? Isn't he her boyfriend?"

"Nah, he's her business partner. And by that, I mean STRICTLY only her business partner." Shelby polished an apple on her sleeve before taking a bite. "Why?" she asked around a mouthful of fruit.

"No reason." He took the apple off his sister and took a

bite. Interesting. Why hadn't Misty corrected him when he'd call Billy her boyfriend?

Noticing he'd eaten down to the core, he made to hand it back to Shelby. She promptly put her hands behind her back. "I don't think so. You know where the worm farm is."

Ambling off to the worms, he mused over Shelby's revelation. Interesting, indeed.

CHAPTER 7

Misty hadn't really given it much thought before she'd agreed to help look after Hope. Seriously, how hard could it be? She'd been around the kid since the day she was born. What she hadn't factored in was two very important things. One, Evelyn had always been there doing most of the mothering, and two, she'd previously cleared her schedule as much as possible while, this time, she'd decided she would still work in a remote capacity while at the ranch. Turns out it wasn't as simple as she'd anticipated.

"How did your meeting go?" Trixie asked from where she was stacking blocks with Hope as Misty plonked down on the sofa.

"Pretty good. The budgets all got signed off." She handed a block to Hope. The little girl, her face the picture of intense concentration, placed it on top of her pile. Misty didn't want to admit that she'd spent way too much time thinking about Logan. "I think it would've been more fun hanging out with you guys. What did you get up to?"

"We hung out the washing and visited Freckles, the pony.

After that, she insisted we swing by her chickens and give them some grass. Then we had lunch and a big nap."

Misty felt a stab of guilt that she hadn't been able to spend as much of the day with them as she would have liked. "Thanks for helping me look after her."

Trixie gave the little girl a quick hug. "She's my little helper."

Misty let out a dramatic groan as her phone began to ring. "For goodness sake," she muttered as she flipped it over. Hadn't she told Dana to hold her calls? It had better be important. Seeing the number, she muttered a few choice words, setting Trixie to give her a reproachful glance.

"Oops, sorry, Hope. Auntie Misty didn't mean to say that. Trixie, I have to take this call." Quickly, she headed to the front porch, closing the door quietly behind her. "Hello, Mom. How much do you need now?"

"Hello, Misty, and I do not appreciate the tone, young lady."

"My apologies. How have you been?" It would be a very novel experience indeed to have a phone call with one of her parents that didn't revolve around them asking her for something—usually money.

"Your father and I have been well. The AC finally got fixed, but we had to wait two days before the man came. Are you sure you couldn't have arranged it faster?" her mother accused. Typical. Even if it didn't cost them anything, there was always something to complain about.

"Actually, it's a really busy time of the year for those repair guys. I had to pay a premium to get him out as fast as I did, but you're welcome," Misty said, her voice heavy with sarcasm. "I assume Dad managed to forget his pain on his fishing charter." She rubbed her forehead. Why did speaking to her parents always leave her on the verge of a migraine? "Well, it's been fun as usual, but I really need to go."

"Brandon's out. He wants to make contact with you."

The words stopped Misty in her tracks. *Out.* She didn't even know if she'd recognize him in the street. A weight dragged down her stomach. "What did you tell him?"

"I told him I'd ask you."

Misty sucked in a breath. At least Mom hadn't handed her details over straightaway. At least, not yet. "Look, Mom, I don't know. I have a lot on at the moment."

"Too busy to talk to your brother? I thought I raised you better, Misty Monroe." Misty bit back the sharp retort that sprung to her lips, agitatedly swinging her legs as she rocked the porch chair. So that's how her Mom wanted to play it? Straight to guilt.

"Well, you raised Brandon too, and he turned out to be a lying, thieving drug addict who caused you to lose everything. I think I didn't turn out that bad in comparison. So, you can get snarky with me all you want, but catching up with him isn't that high on my priorities."

"You've become very disagreeable since we let you move to New York."

Misty gave a sharp bitter laugh. "Is that what you call it? I call it escaping and making a life for myself—one that I've been very successful at. You don't seem to mind it so much when you're asking for money." The dull ache in her head had now reached its full potential and erupted into a migraine, causing her to wince against the light piercing her brain. "Look, Mom, I'm done with this conversation. I'll think about Brandon and I'll let you know what I decide. Goodnight."

She closed her eyes against the pain—if only it was enough to stop the turmoil—she felt at the thought of seeing her brother again. Maybe a bath would dull it to something manageable. With a little groan, she gritted her teeth and staggered back into the house.

~

THE PHONE SAT heavy in his hand, reproachful in its silence. Logan began to type in Misty's number. Heck, he thought it was still her number. She might have changed it since he'd last called her. With a muttered curse, he hung up before he could complete it. It had felt good, real good, in that split second they hadn't been fighting, and then bam, they'd been back at it like cats and dogs. He smiled at the memory, the thrill of adrenaline sparring with Misty always sent coursing through his blood. The fighting wasn't all bad either. It had its own particular brand of spice. It made a fella feel alive.

But that moment when they'd been at peace, there'd been something special about the connection he'd felt to her, a pull to simply breathe her in. He glanced down at his phone. He wasn't even sure if she wouldn't hang up when she heard his voice on the other end. Maybe it wasn't worth risking it. Tossing it onto the passenger seat, he cracked open a can of energy drink and drove into the night.

CHAPTER 8

No sooner had the knots of tension begun to unravel in her shoulders when Misty's time at the ranch was over. Truth be told, with all the long lingering glances and secretive smiles once the newlyweds had arrived home, she'd begun to feel like an interloper and more than a little jealous. Frankly, if they hadn't been so cute, it would have been annoying. She settled into her chair in her office that somehow didn't feel as snug a fit as it had before. Fidgeting, Misty wondered who had been occupying it while she'd been gone. She was on the verge of asking Dana when Chora's smiling face beamed up on her computer screen.

"Misty, how was your break? Didn't she look beautiful?"

"There was no way I was going to let her look any other way." Misty's voice softened with pride. "But yes, she made a beautiful bride." The way her friend had glowed as she'd exchanged vows with the man she loved, it had been a magical privilege to be a part of it. Even if envy niggled at her. "It was great having time on the ranch with Hope, but now it's all hands on deck. It helps that Evelyn has a meeting with a client here in New York tomorrow"—she paused to find the notes she was looking for—"and we're going to have some retail therapy." *Argh, there it was.* Misty snagged the folder sticking out from beneath her planner. "For this upcoming fundraising gala for your charity—it hit me when I saw how beautiful the wedding was at Colt's ranch— instead of having it in a ballroom somewhere, I could host it at my Hamptons estate?"

"The grounds there are gorgeous, and it would give it a different vibe to what we've had the last few years." Chora's eyes gleamed in anticipation, ideas already swirling about by the looks of it.

The thrill of creating pulsed to life in Misty. "We need to do something new then. Something we haven't done before."

Chora leaned forward, her face peering closer into her screen. "And what is that?"

Misty shrugged, scrunching her face up as she laughed. "I have no idea, but leave it with me and I'm sure I'll get some inspiration … eventually."

Her friend shook her head, giggling at her comical expression. "Hopefully before the gala."

"Definitely." *It might be the day before, but that still counted, didn't it?* "Now, I need to wrap this up. I have another meeting I need to get to."

"Of course. I'll keep in touch with any ideas I come up with, too." A quick wave and Chora's face was replaced with a blank screen. Speaking with the animal charity campaigner always left Misty feeling lighter, more energized. Now it was time to put her game face on. She had business to attend to.

"I'm sorry to keep you gentlemen waiting." Misty smiled sweetly—*the better to get them off guard*—as she entered the room. "My other meeting ran late. I assume William has presented our proposal to you?"

Mr Onissios waited for her to take a seat. "He has, and I must say, it is … intriguing."

With a soul-pounding certainty, she knew he was interested in the proposal. It would be the details they would wage polite war over. Misty imposed an iron discipline to not show the elation on her face. "I felt the same way myself when I discovered lotus silk. It has an exciting future ahead."

"I wonder how a company that specializes in tech will have the capabilities to move into the fashion industry." Mr Onissios steepled his fingers, peering at her from over the top of them. "It's a bold move."

"One of the key principles William and I have both implemented in our company is to know our limitations and where to seek outside knowledge. We have the financial resources to put behind this venture. What we don't have, as you so kindly pointed out, is industry experience. But you do."

"I only take on projects I know will be successful." His shrewd gaze locked on hers, the other men in the room relegated to bit players.

Undaunted, she allowed herself a smug upturn of her lips. "So do I."

"How secure is your source of lotus silk?" he countered, shifting his weight to his elbows on the table.

"I have multiple suppliers." Misty mirrored his posture, the thrill of getting closer to closing a deal burning through her veins. "I can also guarantee their financial stability."

"And this would be a joint venture, but my fashion house would be the public face?"

"Yes."

"I will need you to send me enough fabric to work with, say, two rolls."

"It can take a worker two months to weave a scarf," she smoothly objected.

"I need to know if I can work with it. If I am satisfied, we have a deal."

Elation pulsed through her nerves as she calmly rose and extended her hand. "Deal."

As Misty left HQ, she found herself caught up in the crowded Manhattan streets. There was an energy that only existed on these streets. Misty hurried, her heels crisp on the pavement as she made her way to the restaurant she'd made reservations at. Mr Onissios had been quite disappointed when she'd politely refused his invitation to lunch, citing prior plans.

Turning into the foyer of a nondescript apartment block, she turned down a flight of stairs to arrive in a stone floor eatery, a large black granite counter running the length of the tiny space with only fourteen chairs for diners lined up along it. One of those chairs swiveled around, revealing a beaming Evelyn.

Misty rushed forward and pulled her friend into a firm hug. "I hope I didn't keep you waiting." She settled herself on the stool beside her. "How on earth did you know about this place?" She waved at the space around them. "I live here, and I didn't even know it existed."

"I did a sculpture for the owner a few years ago. Whenever he opens a new restaurant, I always get an invitation. When this one opened, Indie had only just died and I wasn't going anywhere and leaving Hope, so when I had my chance today, I decided to come and see it."

"How is Hope? And Colt too, I guess?" A dish was placed down in front of both of them. The food could have passed for art, the composition flawless.

"Hope is happy and healthy back home. Colt is spending more time at the ranch, too. Big Wheel's is having a break to freshen up and then he says he will start back on the circuit again next year."

Misty popped something purple and unidentifiable into

her mouth, surprised at the candied peanut flavor. "I was not expecting that."

"Try the orange stuff," exclaimed Evelyn. "It tastes like a hot dog." Misty happily complied.

It wasn't long before her friend looked at the empty plates in front of them, the latest to fall victim to their ravenous appetite. She glanced at her watch in disappointment. "I guess you need to go back to the office."

Misty slapped herself on the forehead. "How could I forget to mention that I arranged to have the rest of the day off? It's not every day that I get to go shopping with you in New York."

Evelyn's eyes grew huge and she gave an excited clap. "Really? Because Hope needs a whole new wardrobe. She's outgrown nearly everything, and I was planning on buying more while I was here."

"Well then, you're in luck. I happen to know some great shops."

Evelyn raised a dubious brow at her. "Really? You know children's stores here?"

"Well, I know designers who have children's ranges, does that count?"

Her friend laughed in defeat. "You're going to turn her into a designer mini-me of you."

Misty stood and gave a little twirl. "I can't help it if her Auntie Misty knows her fashion. Now, are we just going to talk about shopping or go spend up big on Colt's credit card?"

Happily, Evelyn linked arms with hers. "Show me the way. And as we walk, you can tell me all about what's new with you."

As they headed out into the street, Misty paused to put her shades on. Maybe Evelyn might be able to help her with her current dilemma. "You know the gala I do every year with Chora?"

"Yeah."

"Well, this year I want it bigger and better than ever. I really liked your wedding, and I was thinking of holding it at my Hamptons estate and give it a gentrified country theme."

"I think that sounds amazing." Evelyn had to raise her voice to be heard over the traffic. "Why do I feel like there's a but?"

"Because you know me so well." Misty pouted at her. "I need something memorable—something that hasn't been done before—and I just can't think of anything."

"Um, well, nothing says country like a cowboy." Evelyn's eyes opened wide as inspiration struck her. "I know! You should auction off a date with a real-life cowboy. The society ladies would eat that up."

"Are you offering Colt? Because that might be a little weird." Misty couldn't help teasing.

"Not Colt, silly, but I know just the person." A horrible niggling sensation settled in Misty's belly that turned into a ball of lead at her friend's next word. "Logan."

THE LITTLE COWGIRL clutched the horn of her saddle, giggling as she bounced with each stride of her horse. Logan led the way while Colt jogged beside Hope, holding her in place. Freckles, the pony, kept giving long snorts as if to ask how much longer this was going to be inflicted on him. *You and me both, buddy.*

Finally, Colt called time, and Logan let the pony amble back to the barn and tied him up. Colt gently pulled Hope from the saddle and watched as she toddled over to a stall and began to throw straw about. Somehow, Logan didn't think Trixie would be exactly thrilled when she saw what was trekked back into her spotless house, but he had to give it to the kid. She was one heck of a cute little cowgirl living her best life in the dirt. There was something about the little girl with tiny pink cowgirl boots on that gave Logan a pang, one he sure as heck didn't want to ponder. Breathing in deeply of the pungent livestock aroma that permeated the air, he forced it from his mind.

He was giving the pony a quick rub down when Colt's phone buzzed and his friend began to laugh. "What's so funny?"

Colt only laughed louder as he looked at him, his words jumbled together, mixing with his mirth. "I can't believe she thinks that will work."

Logan narrowed his eyes at his giggling friend. "What will work?"

"You know how Evelyn is in New York meeting with a client?"

"Yeah?"

"Well, obviously she's meeting up with Misty." *Misty.* A tingle shot through him at the mention of her name. "Anyway, she just suggested that Misty auction a cowboy off for her big fundraising gala." Colt began to laugh again. Logan didn't like where this was going. "And the cowboy she suggested was you." His friend pointed a finger dead at his chest.

"No." Logan held out his hands to ward him off. "No way."

"Yes way. Don't be such a sissy. It's for a good cause, and Evelyn wants you to do it. We both know there's something between you and Misty."

"No, there isn't." The denial sprung hot to his lips. *Something* didn't even half describe what it was between them, and darn if he could figure out what it was.

"Well, Evelyn has a theory that you're going to end up with each other."

"Has she told Misty about this theory of hers?" Logan spluttered indignantly. He could only imagine the choice words she'd said in retaliation.

"Not as far as I know. For what it's worth, I have a wager with her that she's wrong." He peered closer at his friend. "She is wrong, isn't she?"

"Of course she's wrong. Misty and I get along about as well as sunburn and hot sauce. What did you wager?"

Colt smirked at him. "That's between me and my wife. But I do want to collect sooner rather than later, and I think you doing this with Misty will end in disaster." The calculating gleam in his friend's eyes was softened by the laughter still lingering there. "In fact, to sweeten the deal, if you do it, I'll give you that gold sportscar I bought last year."

"The one you won't even let me sit in?"

"Yep."

"Deal."

Logan held out his hand to shake on it before his friend could change his mind. That car was worth more than he made in ten years, and all he had to do was stand beside Misty while she sold him to whichever rich lady wanted to go on a date with him. How hard could it be? Where Misty was concerned, those were famous last words.

CHAPTER 9

*M*isty thoughtfully traced the outline of the marquee on the screen of her tablet, considering the lines of the structure and lighting placement. "And you're sure this will be suitable for the number of guests I am hosting?"

"Yes." The event planner nodded, her long earrings bobbing about her face. "I would go so far as to say it's the perfect size. Big enough that, in a pinch, you could fit a few last-minute attendees in, but not so big that you'll lose the intimacy that you want for an event like yours."

"All right, let's book that one in. But I'm still not sold on the color schemes you've given me. I'd like to see three more versions by the end of next week." She gestured at the tablet. "These feel flat, fake. It really needs to capture the sense of the country coming to the Hamptons and not in a cartoon kind of way."

"Of course, I'll have new mood boards to you by midweek."

Misty smiled at her, not missing the woman promising to deliver results earlier than she'd requested. "That would be greatly appreciated." She walked the other woman back out to reception before returning to her office. Standing there with hands on hips, she looked out the expansive floor-to-ceiling panes of glass at the vista below. She could see the traffic snaking through the grid-like streets, imagining the exhaust fumes and cantankerous cab drivers.

"Misty, I have a call for you," Dana's voice said over the phone speaker.

Sighing, she pulled herself away from looking down at the lives playing out below her. "Who is it?"

"He says his name is Brandon, that he's your brother." The information was imparted tentatively as if to test the validity of the claim.

Misty sucked on the inside of her cheek, uncertain what to do. Once—a long time ago—her and Brandon had been tight, and she'd idolized him. But that was before he'd gone down the path he did and chose to hurt everyone he cared about. Before she could change her mind, she picked up the receiver. "Put him through."

"Hello?" His voice sounded different, raspier, tired.

"Hello, Brandon, did Mom give you my number?" She should've known that she'd hand it over, no matter what she'd said.

"No, I googled you and the name of your company came up. And then it was only a matter of searching for the number online."

She sniffed, slightly mollified. "So, I see you're out. Again."

A surprisingly pleasant laugh rumbled down the line. "Yeah." She could hear the smile in his voice. "This time it's for good."

"I think you said that last time." Heck, she'd even ponied up the money to help him get back on his feet and have a new start.

"I wasn't ready last time. There were still a lot of things I needed to work through. I finally admitted I had a problem, and I joined a twelve-step program for addicts and that really helped me see why I did the things I did, why I reacted how I did and, most importantly, how much I hurt the ones I loved the most. I even finished my high school diploma so I could help other people. You know, show them they can do it, too."

This was a side Misty couldn't remember ever seeing. When he spoke, there was a fire in his words. "It sounds … admirable. So, you're going to be a drug counselor?"

"Some of the time. More like when they need me to go talk at schools and stuff. But while I was on the inside this last time, I really discovered that I enjoy cooking. I'm going to try to get some experience in kitchens and then go to culinary school. I mean, I used to cook, but none of that was legal." He gave an uncomfortable cough. "That's all I really wanted to say to you. I understand why you would be hesitant to believe anything I have to say after what I put you and our parents through."

So much pain, that somehow, hearing him describe it tritely as *put you through*, it didn't do it justice. "There was a lot, Brandon."

"Yeah, and I can't take it back. All I can do is say that I'm sorry and prove that I'm working to become a better person and someone you would want to call your brother."

"I can't promise I'll ever want to do that," Misty replied flatly. There was no way she was ever going to let him in again. He'd let her down way too much in the past.

"Look, I'll give you my number"—he rattled off some digits—"if you change your mind and ever want to hear from me."

The line went dead before Misty could formulate a response. Numbly, she let the receiver fall from her fingers, her brain struggling to process the emotions that churned inside her. It was only then that she realized she hadn't written the number down. She didn't know if she was relieved or upset. Deciding that she wouldn't be able to focus on work after that call, she picked up her Hermes bag, gave her excuses to Dana and walked away as fast as her red-soled heels would take her in search of wine.

Balancing her phone on her shoulder later, Misty squinted, trying her best to line up the bottle opener with the cork "Hshlo.".

"Um, Misty are you drinking?" Evelyn asked.

"Only a shimbleful." She crowed in triumph when she hit her target.

"How many shimbles are there in a bottle?"

"About the shame."

"So, you've drunk a bottle then.' Why did it matter so much to her friend?

"I've had three."

"And you're by yourself?"

"Yep." She put the bottle between her knees and began to work on the cork. The sucker wasn't giving up without a fight.

"Hmm, maybe I should call William and have him come and check on you."

"Don't be such a party pooper. I'm just chilling, kinda wish I was grilling, that would be thrilling, but I'm not feelin'." Misty giggled. Gosh, she was clever.

"Okay. Is there anything you want to talk about in particular?"

"Um, Brandon called, and he says he wants to be my brother again and I said, no, no, no." *Wasn't that a song?* The cork gave way, sending Misty flying backwards into her white leather sofa, the contents spilling onto its pristine surface.

"Are you actually singing?"

"Maybe." With extreme concentration. Misty managed to line up the bottle to pour into her glass.

"Do you need me to come out there? Or do you want to come here for a visit? You know, we'd love to have you."

"I'm a big girl."

Evelyn sighed through the phone. "I know you are, but that doesn't stop me from worrying about you. I remember what Brandon did to you and how it hurt."

"Yeah, well, I don't feel anything right now." The wine sloshed as she raised the glass to her lips. Wine. It was going to kick like a mule tomorrow, but tonight it was her best friend.

"Since you're not going to remember any of this tomorrow, I'm going to tell you now and then send you an email. I'm a sadist enough that I kinda enjoy the idea of hungover Misty finding out about this tomorrow."

"You meanie-poo you." *Why was the glass empty again?*

"Yep, that's what I am. Colt spoke to Logan and he agreed to be auctioned off for your charity."

"I don't remember asking him to." *Logan. Handsome, gorgeous Logan. Break-her-heart Logan. Logan...*

"Well, it's done now. Trust me, it's going to raise so much money. Misty? Are you still there? Misty."

A soft snore escaped Misty's lips, the empty glass dangling precariously in her limp hand. Outside her window, the moon glowed dimly through the clouds as the city pulsed beneath it.

THE VIBRATING phone disappeared under the passenger seat. Cussing, fit to make a sailor blush, Logan leaned over and fished it out. There was no caller ID on the display. For a moment, he hesitated, not sure if it was a call he wanted to know about. Throwing caution to the wind, he put it to his ear.

"Hello?"

"Hello, Logan Erikson? This is Dana. I'm Misty Monroe's executive assistant." The woman's voice was crisply professional.

He wondered what she looked like, probably all twin sets and sensible shoes. Probably drinks a lot of coffee to put up with Misty, too. "Hello, Dana. What can I do for you?"

"I've been forwarded your details for the auction. Thank you for supporting such a wonderful cause. I know the founder, Chora, was very excited when she discovered that we have the opportunity this year to have a real-life cowboy attend the event."

No mention of Misty. Probably didn't want to get her hands dirty. Still, it did a man good to hear himself talked about in such a glowing manner. "Thank you, ma'am, it's an honor to be able to help."

"Is there an email address I can forward some paperwork to?"

"Paperwork?"

"Nothing scary," she said, quick to reassure him. "Just some standard contracts about confidentiality and insurance and such."

"Before I sign anything, I'd like to talk to Misty." If she wanted him at her event and raising thousands—no, probably millions—the least she could do was talk to him.

"I think that can be arranged, but unfortunately Misty is feeling ... a little under the weather today. But as soon as she's feeling better, I'll get her to give you a call."

A flicker of concern sparked at her words. "Is she okay?"

"Nothing looking after herself better and a day in bed won't cure."

"Well, in that case, when you tell Misty about calling me, I want you to tell her one more thing. Tell her that my condition for helping is that she's the one who stands beside me and auctions me off." He smirked. Darn, but he wished he could see Misty's face when his demand was delivered. Maybe Colt's gold sportscar had been the bait to get him hooked, but it was the satisfaction of aggravating Misty that kept him on the line. *Yep, I'm sure going to enjoy doing my bit for charity!*

CHAPTER 10

When Misty had woken up, she couldn't shake a sense of unfinished business hanging over her like a miasma. It was one thing to know that Brandon was out of jail, but to hear his voice and how he was attempting to turn his life around, it had rattled her more than she'd care to admit. Lying on her couch, suffering from the aftereffects of her self-medicating session, she came to the grim realization that she was getting too old to solve her problems in the bottom of a bottle. Heck, she'd never been the type, even when she'd been young. Having an addict in the family was pretty persuasive to have a clean lifestyle. There was nothing left to do. She was just going to have to tackle her problem head on. With a groan, she fumbled for her phone, wincing when a loud voice answered.

"Hello, Dana. I'm going to need my plane ready to go in a few hours. Actually, make that at least five hours." Misty swallowed, her tongue sticking to the roof of her mouth. "I need to go to Florida."

Sitting on her parent's sofa that afternoon, the AC blocking any briny fragrance of the ocean outside their condo, Misty was beginning to regret her earlier decision. There were knickknacks and paraphernalia everywhere. At a quick glance, one would assume cheap, but having footed the bill for everything, Misty knew the tawdry look her parents aspired to came with a hefty price tag.

Her mother handed her a glass of water. "I don't understand why you think you're too good to stay with us." She settled herself beside her husband to glare at her daughter. Lined up as they were, it felt like Misty was being interrogated.

Misty schooled her features into a bland, polite expression. "There isn't enough room here, Mom. Your condo only has two bedrooms, and Brandon's staying in the guest room."

"What's this about Brandon?"

Misty wanted to stamp her feet with frustration at her brother's unexpected interruption as he came through the front door, keys in hand. Keys to a condo she'd paid for. *Great, another ally for Mom.*

"Misty was just telling us how the condo she thought was good enough to buy us isn't good enough for her highness to spend the night in to visit us. She's gone and booked herself some fancy hotel."

Her jaw ached from the frozen smile she'd fixed on it. "That's not it at all. Please don't twist my words. I was simply saying there isn't enough room for me to stay."

"You can take my room if you like and I'll take the sofa."

Misty was surprised at his easy offer, as if it were the most natural thing in the world as he took a seat beside her. Somehow it felt like he'd chosen the spot in support of her. She was being silly.

"I don't want to put you out, really, and the hotel is all booked. It's just for the night."

Brandon stared intently at her, then winked with the eye closest to her, shielded from her parents' view. "Actually, I'm pretty relieved you didn't accept my offer. These sofas might look good, but they aren't even that comfortable to sit on. I'm not sure I'd get a great night's sleep out here."

"Brandon!" Mom admonished. "If your sister wants your room, you'll give it."

"But she doesn't want to, Mom, now leave her alone." Misty's jaw went slack at her brother's defense. "It's a really nice evening out there. A perfect temperature for a walk along the beach. Would anyone like to join me?" Although casually asked of the room at large, Brandon's gaze was firmly on Misty.

"You know I don't like sand between my toes." Misty shook her head in disbelief at her father's ungrateful tone, the first words he'd spoken all evening. He'd been the one to insist that he wanted a place within walking distance to the beach.

"Mom?" Brandon turned to their other parent.

"It's so humid out there." Her hand flew to her locks. "You know it wreaks havoc with my hair.

There was a twinkle of amusement in Brandon's dark eyes as they settled on her. "Misty? Any problems with sand between toes or frizzy hair?"

Misty stood up. "Not that I can't live with." She followed him out the door without a backward glance at her parents. This was a side of Brandon she hadn't seen since they were teenagers. Her throat constricted. She'd missed him.

They walked in silence until they reached the sand, the full moon reflected on an inky ocean. Brandon cleared his throat. "I'm glad you came down. Although you might be regretting it now after dealing with Mom and Dad."

Misty laughed. "I'm used to it, but I do still find myself just about bursting a spleen whenever I talk to them longer than five minutes. I don't know how you do it living with them."

"It kinda helps if you don't have a choice in it. It was a condition of my release that I needed somewhere stable to stay." Even in the shadows she could see his expression become somber. "When I was inside, I actually looked forward to their calls. I would tell myself that if I could deal with Mom's complaining, I could deal with anything. But in all seriousness, I'm lucky they even talk to me after what I did to them"—he looked hesitantly at her—"and you."

"Yeah, you weren't exactly son of the year." Misty sucked on her teeth, carefully considering her next words. The sound of her phone ringing made her feel faint with relief. "I'm sorry, I need to get this real quick."

"Sure."

"Hello, Chora."

"Hi, Misty. I just wanted to quickly touch base. I'm about to do a send out to our supporters with a save the date, when I realized I needed to make sure we actually agreed on the date."

"Yes, it's going to be the eighth of September."

"And we're still having it at your place?"

"Yep, at my Hamptons estate. I'm sorry to do this to you, but I'm actually here with my brother. Can I call you back tomorrow?" Misty could see Brandon glance at her from where he stood at the edge of the water, having walked a few yards away to give her privacy.

"Oh, I'm sorry, I didn't mean to interrupt."

"Don't be silly, I didn't have to answer my phone." Misty hung up and walked briskly back to the water. "I'm sorry about that."

"You sound like you're planning one heck of a party."

"It's a charity gala that I'm hosting at my Hamptons estate." Somehow it seemed boastful when she said it to her brother.

"So, lots of guests with deep pockets."

"Well, that's the plan." She chuckled. "It sounds so mercenary when you say it like that, but it's for a really good cause, so that makes it a bit better."

"I'm pretty good at planning." He gave a humble shrug. "It wasn't for nothing that I was the most successful drug dealer in my cell block for several years."

For the second time that evening, Misty's jaw hit the floor. "Um, I'm not sure if that's a selling point or not?"

"All I'm saying is that some of my skill set from my more illegal activities could be transferred over to legit stuff. I'm happy to help if you need it."

"Thanks." And she found herself meaning it. "But I've got it all under control." Her phone buzzed again, a message from Dana flashing on the screen.

Brandon glanced down, the glow from her phone casting shadows on his face. "I think that's our cue to head back. Think of me when you escape back to your nice, peaceful hotel room and I'm left with Mom and Dad." He dramatically threw a hand across his forehead.

Misty gave him a playful push. "You poor thing." Heading back across the sand, her heart felt lighter than it had for years. It was funny, she'd never known how heavy it felt until she didn't have to carry the burden anymore. It was nice to get rid of at least one chip from her shoulders.

MAN, his head hurt. Maybe he was getting too old for this lifestyle. *Nah.* The sun glinted off the windscreen as Logan squinted in the bright midday sun. Last night hadn't gone exactly to plan. A bull he'd thought was going to go right had gone straight instead, leaving him with a pair of cracked ribs for his efforts. It had seemed like a pretty good idea at the time to numb the pain with liquor, but now his body hurt and his brain felt like it was trying to escape his skull.

Spying a sign for the next town, he rubbed at his bleary eyes. Shelby was always telling him that he needed to drink more water. Heck, she even tried to say all the energy drinks and caffeine weren't good for him. Once she'd even made the outlandish claim that eating a piece of fruit or, heaven help him, some vegetables might be good for him. In the bowels of misery, he decided that anything was worth a try.

The small town he stopped in was like so many dotted around the country—the main street a little tired, but still standing. The general store's shelves were adequately stocked as Logan made his way down them, loading up with bottles of water, apples, carrots and bananas. He stopped to peer at what looked like cake rolled into balls. *Bliss balls*, the packaging read, and it even said they were healthy. Maybe this wasn't going to be so bad after all. As he placed the last paper bag in his truck, his phone rang, causing an apple to escape and land on his foot. His pain reflex sent his knee jerking up into the hard metal of his truck, the cell phone falling out of his pocket onto the road. Muttering a few choice words about the inconvenience and pain being inflicted on him by the unknown caller, he knelt, straining to retrieve it from under his truck, all while his cracked ribs screamed in protest.

Triumph made him give a fist pump when he managed to rake it closer with his fingers before safely returning it back into his possession. The movement caused him to smack his head on the under chassis.

"Son of a gun, this better be important." He almost dropped it again when he saw Misty's number. Despite it feeling like someone was using his head for a drum from the inside, a lump already forming to add to it and the agony of his ribs, a slow smile stretched his lips. *Well, I'll be a monkey's uncle. She must really need me for this auction.*

"Misty Monroe as I live and breathe. To what do I owe this pleasure?"

"You know darn well why I'm calling, Logan. You're the one who told my PA that it was one of your demands." He could imagine her mouth all pouty as she huffed at him down the phone.

"It was more of a request, but I'm glad to see that you're taking me seriously. It makes me think that maybe I will help you after all."

"You already said you would." Misty's voice was icy.

"I might be having second thoughts. After all those documents that lady, Dana, sent through, well, it had a lot of things I wouldn't be able to do—or in some cases, I would have to do."

"It's a standard confidentiality contract. Just don't talk about anything sensitive or name names afterwards. And the other document was to hire your services so that we're covered for insurance purposes. But if all the big words scare you, I'm sure we can find someone else."

The question hung there, the silence stretching. Logan wondered if she was biting on her bottom lip, the way she did when she was uncertain if her bluff had been called or not. It was fun pressing her buttons and all, but he had a gold sportscar he needed to become the proud new owner of.

"Look, I'll do it."

"Why?" Suspicion laced the word.

"Because I'm a good person. I like to do my bit, and who am I to stop the ladies bidding on this fine specimen of a man? And I like the idea of you owing me." He waited for her cutting reply. "Hello? Misty?" Son of a gun, she'd hung up on him!

CHAPTER 11

"*D*id you receive the email from Mr Onissios?" William, as fashionable as ever, waltzed into Misty's office. He paused to straighten the vignette on her coffee table before giving a sharp twitch of his cuffs. "I think it calls for a celebration."

How was it even possible that William had managed to read the email and get to her office so quickly? Heck, she'd only just received it herself. "Where did you have in mind?" She picked up her bag, pausing to stroke the soft inky blue.

"Jackman's for a drink. New bag?"

Misty beamed at him happily. When she'd been little, she'd always loved handbags and shoes and the Hermes brand had always been the ones she'd drooled over whenever she'd seen them at fashion shoots or on the arms of celebrities. To now own not one, but several, and to be invited regularly to purchase new ones was beyond her craziest dreams. The fact that each bag cost more than most people's cars was the icing on the cake. It was her badge of having made it.

"Yeah, they sent it over this morning and I just couldn't wait to use it."

"I can't blame you. That color is something else." A low grumble sounded in his belly.

She laughed. "By the sounds of it, you should get something to eat before we start drinking. Actually, I'm feeling a bit hungry myself, and I know just the place." She pressed the elevator button. "I think it might be a new experience for you."

He winked at her. "I'm always up for new experiences."

Misty was remembering his confidence as, minutes later, he stared down in disgust at his chilli dog. The sounds of traffic and humanity filled her senses. "This is not the new experience I had in mind. Maybe Ethiopian or Tibetan, not this"—he poked at the contents of his aluminum foil package —"thing."

"Ah, come on, William, it's not that bad." To prove her point, she took a hearty bite, savoring the burn on her lips. "Just a little nibble."

"It's moments like this that make me really reconsider our friendship." William marched over to the trashcan and threw the offending meal away. "If you weren't so useful to have around, I'd do it too. So you're lucky."

Misty giggled before taking another bite. "Yes, I am, and you know you can't live without me. We're like two peas in a pod."

"Some pod. Now are we going to celebrate or not?"

Smiling, she glanced around and blinked. Startled, she peered at the familiar looking man. "Is it all right if I meet you there?" Without waiting for his reply, she began to walk briskly away.

"Do you want me to wait?' William called after her.

"No." She waved him off. "I'll only be a few minutes behind you."

She grimly pressed on, trailing the man who had turned

with his companion down a seedy-looking alley. Visions of what happened to nice girls in places like that flashed through her mind, but determined, she pressed on. Misty wrinkled her nose against the odor of rotting garbage mingling with the greasy cooking fumes that blew out into her path.

The men stopped, their backs to her near stacks of water-stained crates leaning haphazardly against a rusting dumpster and appeared to pass something between them. "Brandon! What are you doing here? I knew I couldn't trust that you'd changed."

Her brother jerked, bewildered at the sudden accusation she hurled at him. Hurt flashed as he slowly opened his hand to show a packet of cigarettes. The other man glanced at him in question.

"Carl, this is my sister, Misty. Misty, the man who just shared his cigarettes with me is Carl. He's my sponsor."

Misty wondered if it was too much to ask for the pavement to open up and swallow her. "Um, I'm pleased to meet you, Carl." Embarrassed that she'd gotten it so wrong, she attempted to salvage the situation. "Ah, you didn't mention that you were going to be in town, Brandon."

"I'm only here for the day. I need to get back home for my curfew. It's a condition of my parole unless I prove that I'm required to be away for a short period of time due to employment. I'm here to talk to kids about what drugs do to your life and how you can turn it around."

"The kids really engage with him," Carl added. "He's a natural."

Brandon smiled, blushing at the praise. "I'm just happy you think I've made enough change to do it. Thanks for recommending me for it and coming up with me."

Misty watched the exchange, mortified that she'd misjudged the situation so badly. "I'm sorry I jumped to conclusions, but why didn't you tell me you were coming? And why are you in this alley?"

He tapped a cigarette out of the pack and placing it to his lips. "I could ask you the same. And because it's clear—and judging by what just happened here—that you still don't feel comfortable around me or trust me, I didn't need any bad vibes coming into today. I sure as heck didn't think you'd want me anywhere near where you work or your home." The door opened and a kitchenhand appeared, passing a takeout bag to Carl.

Guilt gnawed in her gut at the truth of his words, embarrassed at the assessing look being leveled at her from Carl. "At the least, let me fly you both home on my plane."

Carl looked excitedly at Brandon. Clearly the idea appealed to him. His hopes were, however, quickly dashed. "The tickets have all been paid for. Maybe next time." Her brother lit the end of his cigarette, drawing in deep puffs of smoke like a drowning man.

Misty desperately wanted to make things right. "Do you still want to be a chef?"

He glanced at her suspiciously. "Yeah."

"How about I put in a good word with the caterers for my gala? Maybe you can get some work experience. And you never know what might come from it."

He continued to eye her balefully, dragging on the smoke before a big grin split his face. "If you can arrange it and get it past my parole officer, it'd be great."

Brandon came forward and wrapped her in a nicotine-drenched hug. Holding her breath, she held him back. "And Brandon, I insist you take my town car to the airport when you leave. It's the least I can do."

"We accept," Carl said quickly, obviously scared Brandon would decline.

It wasn't much, but maybe Misty hadn't ruined her chances with her brother after all. Maybe.

THE TABLE WAS BATTLE-SCARRED. Having survived him and Shelby it must have been made of sturdy stuff. Logan traced where the letters he'd written on homework long ago had, over time, been engraved into the timber. It felt like a lifetime ago when his father had surprised his mom with the new piece of furniture. If Logan remembered correctly, outside of their beds, it and the chairs that came with it were the only pieces of furniture they'd had in the house for a long time after they'd bought it. As a kid, all the space had felt like paradise after being cooped up in the old trailer.

"Do you want another helping of pie?" Mom asked, holding it out.

"I don't think I could fit in another bite, Mom, you gave me a huge first helping." As proof, he rubbed his distended belly.

Shelby took the plate from their mother's hands. "Well, I guess it would be a shame to waste it." She dug in heartily.

Logan tilted his head as he looked at her. She was tall. Maybe she put all the food away in her hollow legs. "You could've saved it for Dad."

"Why? He gets Mom's cooking all the time."

His mom swatted him on the arm with a dishtowel. "Leave her alone. One day I might even fatten her up a little."

He grinned at her. "Like a prize heifer."

"Mom!" Shelby protested, glaring at her brother. "You did not just call me a cow."

"Logan, stop calling your sister livestock." His mom's shoulders shook with suppressed laughter as she gave them both a longsuffering look before looking at their father. "Can you talk to your children?"

"He tried when we were kids, it didn't really stick. It's why I'm on the road all the time—to get away from Shelby."

"And it's why I left home—so I didn't have to see him when he finally returned," Shelby agreed pleasantly, spooning more pie into her mouth.

"Logan, Shelby, that's not true," their mother admonished. "We might not have had much, but I raised both of you to love and respect your family."

Logan stood and gave his mother a kiss on the cheek. "We're just funning, Mom."

"Yep," agreed Shelby, crumbs falling from her mouth. "Anyway, he's just sore that only old ladies are going to bid on him at the auction." Horrified, she stared at him. "Are you going to have to kiss them?" She puckered up and made kissy faces at him.

Mom ruffled his hair. "Well, I think he's going to make lots of money for the charity." She beamed at him in pride. "How could he not? He's such a handsome young man, isn't he, Father?"

His dad looked at him, giving a slow nod. "Yep, them old ladies are going to eat him alive."

"Dad!" Logan protested, sending Shelby into fits of giggles.

"Ignore your dad. Now, what are you going to wear?" She began to clear the plates away. "You have that nice shirt I got you for Christmas, the one with the blue stripes. Or what about the one you wore as Colt's best man?"

Shelby snorted. "And just think about it, you'll already be dressed for a wedding if the old lady gets any ideas about matrimony."

Logan gave her his best side eye. It was bad enough that Misty was going to parade him around town like some sort of prize bull in the lead up to her fancy gala. Heck, that was enough to give him a sleepless night before he left in the morning, but his sister didn't need to lay it on so thick about the old ladies. Maybe he'd get lucky and a beautiful, young billionairess might bid on him. He sighed. *In his dreams.*

The tarmac was sleek with rain that had fallen for the last half hour of the flight as Logan stepped out the hatch and onto the stairs, overnight bag in hand. He'd always pegged Misty as showing off since she'd bought a private plane. She sure did seem to mention it a lot at any rate. After having experienced the luxurious comfort he'd just traveled in, well, it would be easy to get used to. Pulling his fleece-lined denim jacket snug about his body, he surveyed his surrounds, watching as a black town car pulled up near the base of the plane. The driver stepped out, umbrella in hand to shield his passenger. *Man, Misty really had become precious.*

At least she came herself. Smiling smugly, he began to make his way down the steps, whistling a jaunty tune. The driver opened the door and a black leather boot clad leg emerged. Logan's smile deepened. There was something about a shapely leg clad in a high leather boot that just did something to a man. He didn't think Misty was the type, but heck, he wasn't going to complain. The umbrella was raised as she stepped out, revealing blonde hair and a face that was older than he'd been expecting. His steps faltered.

"Mr Erikson?" The blonde came forward, her driver anxiously hovering over her like a mother hen.

"Yeah." Logan wasn't at all happy about the disappointment that settled like a stone in his belly. *So what if it wasn't Misty.* It didn't stop visions of her wearing thigh-high boots shimmying around his thoughts.

"I'm Dana, I believe we spoke on the phone." There was an appreciative gleam in her false eyelash bordered eyes. Logan found himself returning it with a slow smirk of his own. It appeared that Dana might be a warm-blooded cougar under the cool voice he'd heard on the phone. "Misty has requested I take you shopping before I escort you to your accommodation for the week."

With a thud, he set his overnight duffle on the tarmac at his feet. "I have everything I need here."

She looked down, unimpressed at what she saw, and raised a dubious brow at him. "Where is the rest of it?"

"That's it. I travel light."

"Not for the engagements you'll be attending this week."

"Look lady," he began.

"Dana," she coolly interjected.

"I'm sorry, Dana, there's no need for the expense of a shopping trip. I'll make do with what I've got."

"You're a corporate expense now." She gestured for the driver to pick up the duffle. Logan quickly took the umbrella and held it over her as they made their way to the car. "Besides, I haven't had a man to shop for in quite some time."

Logan gave her his best smoldering look. "I find that hard to believe."

"It's sadly true. There's a shortage of older men who want age-appropriate women in New York."

"I'm sure there are plenty of younger men who would be

more than happy to share your company." Logan wondered who was doing it for Misty. Probably that William. There wasn't any way she was lacking for male companions. "Now, Miss Dana, if I let you take me shopping, will I still have my boots and hat on by the end of it?"

She gave a naughty giggle. "I can't guarantee it, but I promise I won't let anything bad happen to you."

Logan found himself blushing under her knowing gaze. "I'll put myself in your capable hands then." Feeling slightly like the lamb being led to the slaughter by a smiling cougar, he followed her to the car.

A short time later, men who were prettier than women and women who made his head spin swirled around him like exotic butterflies. Problem was, he felt more like a cactus flower than a rose. He'd expected a visit to the mall, not this brightly lit, sparsely furnished boutique. The shelving that was dotted randomly about the space were backlit, making him feel like he was in some sort of spaceship.

Curiously, he turned over the tag hanging from his sleeve, spluttering when he saw the price. How much was Misty planning on spending on him? Disgruntled, he stared at himself in the mirror, the garish purple shirt making him want to blink. No man he knew would wear a shirt that shade, not to mention the silver gray slim fit trousers it was tucked into. What the heck was Misty trying to do? He was more than a little offended that she thought he needed to change. Heck, there wasn't anything wrong with the original. It's been just fine for him to be offered the gig.

Dana, picking up on his vibe, waved a hand at the buzzing attendant. "Thank you, that'll be enough. I don't think this is quite the look we're going for." She rested her chin thoughtfully in her hand. "But I know what is."

Logan didn't know whether to be afraid or relieved. All

he knew was that when he got his hands on Misty, he was going to give her one heck of a piece of his mind.

~

MISTY COULD HEAR Dana's throaty laughter before the elevator door even opened. *What the heck? Was that Jeremy laughing, too?* It had been months since her chef had still been there when she'd come home from work. Normally he prepared the meals and was long gone before she finally managed to drag herself home. He'd adapted to satisfying his urge to nag her via notes.

"—and just when I thought he had me, I jumped headfirst into that drum. I swear, when I came out, he'd plumb taken my pants off me and I was as naked from the waist down as the day I was born."

Logan held his hand solemnly to his chest. Jeremy was on the edge of his seat—well, Misty's sofa—and the way Dana gazed at Logan in open adoration made Misty roll her eyes. It was galling how she felt like she was intruding in her own home. Or maybe it was how he seemed a perfect fit in her private sanctuary.

"Well, that's one way to give the bull something to aim for," Misty muttered sourly, putting her bag down, noticing the empty bottles of wine. It seemed everyone was having a party at her expense and she wasn't even invited. Heck, they hadn't even seemed to notice she was standing in her own apartment yet.

"You have such an exciting life being a rodeo clown." Jeremy topped up Logan's glass. *Sure, give him more of my wine. It's only eight hundred dollars a bottle, and I'm sure he'll appreciate the vintage.* Sourly, she watched him quaff it down.

"We prefer to be called Rodeo Protection Athletes. I only wear over-the-top clown makeup when I'm acting as the barrel man." He took another gulp of wine to her disgust. "Now, a barrel man, he provides the comic relief."

"Sounds like you're perfect for the part," Misty muttered under her breath as she poured herself a glass. It sure as heck didn't appear like anyone else would. Logan appeared to choose to ignore her, but both Dana and Jeremy sent her frowning looks of disapproval.

"Anyway, I prefer to be one of the bull fighters. In fact, I'm the current American bull fighting freestyle champion." Misty was surprised that this was the first she'd heard about it. Was it even a thing? Maybe she didn't know as much about him as she thought. No, she knew everything she needed to, thank you very much!

Dana looked like she'd just found out he was an Olympic gold medalist. "Wow, you must be really good to win that."

"Yeah, but I was lucky. All the guys were amazing athletes, but on the day, the luck went my way." He drank down the last of his wine, and Jeremy went to refill it only to find the bottle empty.

Misty sent him a level look. "Oh, did I drink the last of my wine? The bottles that no one bothered to ask me if it was okay? You do remember whose place this is, right?"

Dana looked guilty. "I didn't think it would be an issue," she stammered.

Logan simply looked defiant, as if it was his right to have her people fawning over him. "Nice place."

"Yeah, I like it. But considering what I paid for it, I'd say I'm pretty fond of it."

Misty knew she sounded petty, but Logan had a way of making her feel like she needed to jump up and down to get attention. She swallowed down her irritation, along with a mouthful of wine, and left them to it. She could feel their startled gaze as she stomped to her bedroom. Slipping her pumps off was pure bliss. Misty wiggled her toes into the plush carpet, rolling her shoulders to relieve the tension.

A knock at the door had them tensing up again. The door opened to reveal Logan lounged indolently against the frame, those piercing pale blue eyes lazily taking in her and the bed behind her. She was by no means blind to his attraction. It had always been her curse.

"They're gone," he drawled.

Misty looked around—anything to stop the tingle that was growing in the pit of her stomach—and spied the bags of shopping in the hall behind him. "I trust Dana made sure you have suitable attire."

"Yeah, looks like I'm costing you a fortune."

"You better be worth it." *Gosh, she sounded like a peevish old woman.*

Logan winked at her, the air of arrogance around him maddening. "You know I'm worth it or I wouldn't be here."

Misty's belly rumbled in protest at her neglect breaking the moment. Deep grooves ran down each side of Logan's mouth as he laughed, the mirth reflected in his gorgeous eyes. "I see you still need to be fed often."

"These days it seems to only happen when my stomach reminds me that I need to. Have you eaten?"

"No, I think your friends were trying to get me drunk, but they have obviously never drunk with a Texan cowboy. I could kill for a burger right about now."

She looked at her bare feet, weighing up if going out to get food was worth having to put her shoes back on. With a sigh, she reached out for them. She already knew the answer. "I know just the place."

The look on his face as she led him past the line into the obviously very expensive and very exclusive restaurant was priceless. "Are you sure you're just allowed to waltz on past everyone?" he whispered. "This doesn't look like a burger joint."

"Trust me," she whispered back. Ignoring the glares of the fashionably dressed they bypassed on their way to the front of the queue.

"Ah, Ms Monroe, a pleasure as usual," the concierge greeted her. "Will you be wanting your usual table?"

"Yes, Manuel, but I'm just going to slip back to the kitchen and say hello to Gunter first."

"Of course." He stepped discreetly to the side. "You know the way."

Logan was still giving her a baffled look. Clearly he thought she'd either lost her marbles or was pulling a prank on him. Maybe both. "You need to trust me. This guy is a Michelin starred chef, but he also makes the best burgers. You just have to ask him nicely."

The kitchen was a hive of activity. Gunter was at the center of it, barking orders and seemingly everywhere at once. Spying the interlopers in his domain, he came over and kissed both cheeks.

"Ah, Misty. Let me guess, you have special friend at last, and you want me to make you a beautiful three course meal. That I can do for you, my lovely."

Misty's face burned brightly, something Logan seemed to find extremely intriguing given the sharp focus in his gaze. Mortified, she tried to regain control of the situation. "Gunter, this is Logan, and he never has been and never will be my special friend. But I have known him a long time, and he doesn't believe me that you make the best burgers in New York."

Gunter pulled himself up to his full height of a smidge over five feet tall. "I pick up the gauntlet you have cast at my feet. Challenge accepted. Now, Misty, get out of my kitchen."

"Yes, Gunter."

She quickly ushered Logan away before the mercurial chef could make any more awkward predictions. Weaving through the white cloth-covered tables, she finally made it to the private table set at the back and slightly out of view of the other diners. Hushed conversations floated like little clouds over each group, the air filled with expensive fragrances that cost more per ounce than gold. It was the smell of elitism and wealth. Misty wasn't oblivious to the raised brows and mocking expressions of the men they passed nor the dreamy sighs and naked longing from the women for Logan.

He surprised her by blocking the path of the waiter that materialized and instead held out her chair himself. She was too startled to offer any objection, instead sliding into the proffered chair. "Thank you."

"May I get both of you a drink?" The waiter neatly side-stepped Logan as he took his own chair.

"I'll have a beer and the lady would like a cosmopolitan"—Logan raised his brow—"that is, if she still drinks them."

"A cosmo will be fine." With a swift nod, the waiter scurried away. A warm little glow flooded her as a memory flared to life. Logan swearing he knew how to make cocktails and the only thing he'd been able to make that was at least a bit drinkable had been cosmopolitans. Indie, Evelyn and her had thought they were so sophisticated sipping them.

The cowboy took in the array of implements in front of him. "I may need a little assistance if you expect me to try to eat a burger with all this."

The corner of her mouth twitched at the image of him wrestling with the cutlery as he cut the burger into dainty bite-sized morsels. "I think we can skip it tonight, but there will be some functions this week that will be a full silver service." Guiltily, she hadn't considered that Logan might not have ever been exposed to the intricacies. "Don't worry, I'll make sure you know what's what."

"I'd be mighty obliged."

She shook her head laughingly at him. "You don't need to lay it on so thick with me. I'm not the people we're trying to impress."

Logan's stare was bold and frankly assessing. "Maybe I want to impress you."

She was saved from having to answer him with the arrival of dinner. Anxiously, she waited while he picked at it. "It's always a good sign when it needs two hands." Misty tried to stop the blush creeping up her neck as she thought about what else that could be applied to. He seemed to read her mind and gave her a naughty wink. Taking a bite, he closed his eyes to savor it.

"They're good, aren't they?"

Logan opened those magnetic eyes of his. "They're pretty good, almost as good as what you can get back in Texas. Of course, if you tell anyone I said that, I'll deny it."

Misty laughed, caught up in the moment. "I promise not to tell." As she tucked into her own burger, he made no attempt to hide the fact he was watching her. Self-consciously, she dabbed at her chin with a napkin, his compelling gaze riveting her to the spot. "Do I have something on my face?"

"No."

Her skin prickled pleasantly, as if she could feel his gaze caress her skin. "Why do I have a feeling that any moment now you're going to say something and I'm going to go back to disliking you intensely?"

"Maybe because you're always looking to be offended by me. Misty, I spend most of the time laughing at life. Maybe you shouldn't always take everything so seriously."

His words hurt more than she cared to admit. "I guess

that's what we always come back to," she retorted quickly over her choking heart.

"Why am I staying at your place? You could afford to put me up in any hotel in this city and not have me underfoot irritating the living heck out of you. So why there?"

Misty found herself trapped by the intensity in his gaze. The expression putting lie to him not taking anything seriously. "It's the only way I can keep an eye on you and make sure you'll go to all the events I need you to." It was close enough to the truth. She did want to keep an eye on him, she just wasn't sure if the gala was her sole motivation. "Look, it's getting late, and I have a lot to do tomorrow."

Logan pushed back his chair. "It's been a long day for me, too. Shopping plumb wears a man out."

He came over to Misty's side of the table and pulled her chair out as she rose. A waiter bustled past, causing Logan to take a step forward just as she stood. She could smell his aftershave as she found herself perilously close to his broad chest. Heart pounding, Misty remembered what it had felt like to be held close to it. As he stepped back and gestured for her to precede him, she chastised herself for being stupid. *Don't fall for his charms. Look what happened last time.* She took some solace in the fact that they couldn't go longer than five minutes without fighting like cats and dogs. As they stepped out into the chill of the evening, Misty glumly considered the long week ahead of her with the cowboy.

CHAPTER 13

"Is he not the manliest thing you've ever seen?" Gustav, the hairstylist, fluttered his eyelashes outrageously at the object of his affection. "He can park his boots under my bed any day."

"I could just stare at him all day." Liz, the colorist, sighed as she clutched a hair chart to her chest. "That jaw looks like it could be carved from pure granite. He should be in the movies."

"I'd pay to see anything he's in," agreed the young apprentice sweeping the floor near them.

If Misty could hear it from her vantage point beside Logan, then she knew he sure as heck could too. Given the twitching of his lips and the blatantly smug side glances he was casting her way, he wanted to be sure she heard it. Frankly, the conversation made her want to be sick. Seriously, he was handsome, but in New York, handsome men were a dime a dozen.

Gustav, having finish his indiscreet appraisal of his new client, sauntered back over, scissors and various tools of his trade hanging from his hip like a modern-day follicle cowboy. He stood behind Logan and ran his hands through his hair experimentally. "Liz, what are your thoughts? Highlights?"

Liz took her place at his side, staring at Logan's reflection in the mirror. "The natural light caramel tones he has in his hair are quite nice. I'm thinking maybe a few lighter highlights to contrast with it."

The hairdresser peered at the mirror. "I'm thinking a slightly modern take. It's getting a little scruffy. We want to keep that wild manly look but give him a slightly more polished veneer. A little height on top and shorter sides, a little texture."

"Maybe while you're at it, you could give his eyebrows a little tidy up. Wax them," Misty suggested, smiling sweetly at Logan's horrified expression that threatened retribution at a later date.

"Oh my, no," cried Gustav. "Their boldness frames his spectacular eyes. It would be a crime to tamper with them." The gushing praise made her want to gag. She wondered why she was even there and hadn't insisted that Dana chaperone him.

"I'm glad that you appreciate the form you have to work with." Logan's words might have been directed at the hairstylist, but the smirk was all for Misty. "You have no idea how hard it's been for me."

"Dana will be in to take you to your next appointment, so I'll leave you in Gustav's capable hands." Misty pushed herself off the table she'd been leaning against beside the mirror. The panicked look her words elicited was slightly gratifying.

"What do you mean next appointment? And where are you going? I thought I was your project today."

She reached out and cupped his cheek, ignoring the thrill that touching him sent coursing through her. "Logan, I've delegated you as a project to Dana for the rest of the day as my time is better spent doing actual work. Oh, and your next appointment is for body waxing and a spray tan. Gotta have you in peak condition if I have any hope of getting good money for you at the auction." Logan blinked as she patted his cheek for added emphasis, his eyes wide at her words. "But don't worry, I'll be back in plenty of time to make sure you're ready exactly to my specifications for the dinner we're attending tonight. After all, I can't have my prized cowboy wearing just any old thing."

Whistling, she strolled out of the salon. It wasn't often that she left a sparring match with Logan feeling like she had the upper hand, so she was going to enjoy every last second of it. Before she forgot, she sent a message through to Dana informing her of the change of plans and asking if she could babysit Logan for the day. After all, it most definitely hadn't been the plan when they'd set out that morning.

By the time she pressed send, Misty was feeling rather pleased with how the morning had ended after its gag-inducing beginning. Looking around, she saw an old man sitting on a bench watching the people pass, a coffee in his hand as he fed the birds. Everywhere people were walking briskly in the cool air, energized as they went about their business under a bright blue sky. It really was a marvelous day. Thinking the ping that sounded on her phone was Dana returning her message, she glanced down only to discover it was from her caterers. Smiling, she dialed her brother.

"Hello, Misty." It sounded like she might have woken him. She shrugged. If she was living with their parents, she'd probably try to sleep most of it away, too.

"Hi, Brandon. I know it's late notice, but I gave all your details to the caterers and they say they have a position for you at the event. It's just helping set up and pack up and then busboy on the day, but it is paid. I made sure they weren't going to get free labor from you."

"Wow, thanks, Misty. I'll need to get all the details and give it to my parole office." Gosh, it was good to hear her brother upbeat and enthused.

"I can send all that through. And I was thinking, you're more than welcome to stay at my place in the Hamptons. There's more than enough space and I'd really like having you there." The offer that had begun tentative firmed up as she found she meant it.

"Let me talk to the caterers and parole officer and see what they all say. Can I let you know?"

"Yes." She glanced at her watch. "I'll give you a call in a few days and we can discuss it then. I just wanted to give you the good news."

"Thanks, Misty. It means a lot."

Smiling, she said her farewells and hung up the phone. It really was, quite simply, a good day to be alive.

HAVING ESCAPED the overly protective clutches of the attentive Dana, Logan had set off to explore the city. They weren't kidding when they called New York a concrete jungle. Logan was more than aware that, if he lived in the city, there was no way he could afford to be Misty's neighbor. He wasn't dense. He knew she was disgustingly rich. But to be surrounded by it, immersed in how she actually lived, well, it was intimidating how much Misty had. It was clear as daylight that she didn't need a man to provide for her, so what on God's green earth could he offer a woman like that? He shook his head to dispel the unsettling notion that he was even thinking about her in that light. Their entire history had made it quite obvious that they could never be at a truce for very long. Didn't stop a man from wondering what it would be like.

As he set his feet for home, he tried to imagine living here with Misty. Who was he kidding? He'd be like a horse that never got time in a field, restless and looking to make trouble. Nope, he needed wide open spaces and to be able to breathe clean air. Before he knew it, he was greeting the uniformed footman and making his way to Misty's private elevator. Logan was somewhat startled when she greeted him clad only in a robe.

She stiffened, a stain of scarlet appearing on her cheeks. "I thought you were someone else." Misty crossed her arms over her chest, making the robe gape temptingly. "Anyway, you were meant to be back here ages ago."

Jealousy darkened his vision. "Well, darlin', I'm here now and he isn't," he drawled, stepping slowly into her space. He could see her pupils dilate, but she held her ground as she stared at him in burning reproach.

Misty opened her mouth, but before her stinging rebuttal could be delivered, the elevator door opened with several people wheeling cases and a clothing rack appeared. Relief washed over her features as she peered past him.

"Excellent timing. I'll be getting ready in my room, if you'd like to come with me." Without so much as another glance in Logan's direction, she spun on her heel and ushered them into her private sanctuary. The last thing he glimpsed was a swish of fabric and a shapely calf and then the door clicked shut. All he could do was breathe in her fragrance that lingered in the emptiness she had left behind. An emptiness that always kept him running.

With a muttered curse, he grabbed a beer from the wine refrigerator, pausing at the sight of his favorite brand sitting among the craft beer, cider and wine. He didn't recall her being much of a beer drinker and he didn't imagine William would drink anything that common. So who the heck was she keeping beer on hand for? Cracking the can open, he chugged it down, jealous of the nameless man—one who Misty obviously cared for. Well, he was here, and that other guy wasn't. More importantly, he was the one who was helping Misty with her gala. Finishing the beer, he headed for the shower. She wasn't the only one who knew how to dress all fancy.

Several hours later, when his dress shirt was beginning to feel too tight and he'd adjusted his belt for the umpteenth time. The door to her room swung open and, with as much acknowledgement as they'd given him when they'd entered, the gaggle of eclectically dressed people departed.

"Well, it was great meeting y'all, too," he said, raising his beer to the closed elevator doors.

"Are you talking to me?"

Logan's head swung around at Misty's quietly spoken words, his jaw dropping open at the vision in front of him. She'd been beautiful as she'd walked down the aisle at Colt and Evelyn's wedding, but now she looked like something that had stepped straight out of a magazine. Now she looked smoking hot.

The way the form-fitting red capelet dress hugged her curves whilst they were still hidden from view made a man wonder what she'd look like out of it. Misty peered at him intently, the look in her eyes at odds with the haughty tilt of her chin. He looked at her like he was committing her to his memory—and maybe he was. After this week was over, they'd both return to their running battle whenever they happened to run in to each other at Colt and Evelyn's ranch. Logan knew she was waiting for him to say something.

"You look beautiful." Her answering smile made his knees weak.

"You don't scrub up half bad yourself."

"Why, thank you, ma'am." He tilted an imaginary hat in her direction. After much debate, he'd decided to appease himself with only wearing his cowboy boots with the getup Dana had selected for him. He offered his arm to her. "Shall we go?"

For the briefest of moments, Misty hesitated, and then laid her hand tentatively on his arm. Through the fabric of his sleeve, Logan could feel the warmth of her skin. The reaction to her touch was swift, his heart hammering in his chest as he studied her profile, trying to calm his senses. Her mouth curved in an unconscious smile, and he wondered if she knew how gorgeous she was. *Probably.* Misty turned to him, her eyes bright with the pleasure of his attention. Or, at least, he hoped that was why.

"We're as ready as we're ever going to be." Personally, Logan wasn't sure.

The feeling still gripped him as they exited the town car and made their way up the brownstone mansion's steps. Logan could see the edge of Central Park from his vantage point at the top of the steps as they waited for the butler to admit them.

Once they were, Logan wasn't sure if it had been worth the wait. He'd much preferred the less rarefied air outside. This didn't look like the country Texas style wealth that Colt chose to display, nor the luxury of Misty's penthouse. This was elegant old money décor, from walnut furniture to the oriental rugs on the floor. It was understated, no more in common with gawdy new money as a cashmere sweater was to a white chinchilla fur coat.

"Membership to join this club is so exclusive that you can't buy your way in no matter how wealthy you are." Misty whispered discreetly to him as they made their way over to the hosts.

"You've gained entry into it," he noted, suddenly feeling

like a country bumpkin for the first time since he'd arrived in New York.

"No, I'm an outsider. But"—she leaned in closer, and Logan could smell the heady notes of her perfume—"they love to be seen supporting charities, and I happen to host one of the biggest charity galas on the society calendar."

"Ah, Misty, so glad you could make our little soiree tonight." A rail thin, perfectly coiffured blonde woman greeted them. "Harrison, isn't it marvelous Misty could make it?"

"Indeed, it's always a pleasure, Misty. Now, if you'll excuse me, I see Hamilton and I simply must catch up with him. He owes me a game of tennis and he's a nightmare to get a hold of this time of year." Without further preamble, the balding Harrison was gone. On the whole, it had been rather disconcerting, the man having never once looked in Logan's direction, instead directing his attention to Misty.

"Thank you for inviting us, Barbara. This is Logan." She rested her hand lightly on his arm. In another circumstance —and with any other woman—he would have seen it as a possessive gesture. No matter Misty's motive, her touch sent electric shocks tingling along his nerves as it usually did. "He's kindly allowing us to put him up for auction at the gala."

The pearl-wearing Barbara inspected him like Logan suspected she appraised her horses—and men, for that matter. "I can think of a few ladies who will be bidding quite high for him. Is he really a cowboy? Or"—she gestured at his boots—"is it just for show?" She crossed her hands over her heart. "You can tell me your secret."

"Ma'am, I'm as close to the real thing as you can get. Just a few days ago, I was outrunning a bull in Cheyenne." Logan gave her his best smoldering smirk. She wanted cowboy, she was going to get cowboy.

"Oh my," she twittered. "If I didn't have Harrison, I'd be tempted to bid myself."

He lowered his voice to a silky drawl. "Maybe it could be our little secret."

Misty's grip firmed on his arm. "Okay, I think Logan and I will circulate and talk to some of your other guests." She positively dragged him away.

"I thought I handled that well," Logan congratulated himself aloud.

Misty's fingers dug into his skin, a polite cool smile fixed on her face like a mask. "Here's the rules for tonight. Keep it vague, keep it civil and for heaven's sake, don't rock the boat."

"Trust me, I'll be so discreet you won't even know I'm here."

"Well, you also need to impress the ladies. They're the ones, after all, who are going to bid for you." Somehow, she'd gained the marvelous trick of speaking without her lips moving. Logan was impressed. Misty truly was a woman with hidden talents.

"Be discreet, but flirt with the ladies who have money and look lonely." He rolled his shoulders, trying to loosen the grip his shirt had on him. "Got it."

"But don't flirt too much, otherwise they'll think I hired some sort of male gigolo." Misty nodded at several women they passed.

"I hear gigolos make a good living." Logan quite enjoyed the way her ears were turning a delicate shade of pink. Clearly she wasn't finding this conversation as amusing as he was.

"Behave."

"We both know that's never been my strong suit."

"Well, try," she ground out from behind clenched teeth,

her smile not slipping once. "Ah, William, have you been here long?"

"I only just arrived." Misty's business partner took several glasses of sherry from a waiter, handing one to Misty first, then surprising Logan by handing him another and finally taking one for himself. "You know how I feel about these types of events."

"I do, and thank you for coming. Can you excuse me a moment? There's Charlotte Fairhurst and I need to speak to her about a couple of things." Misty leveled a hard look at Logan, clearly warning of dire action if he misbehaved. He gave her his best lazy smile, one that said he wasn't promising anything. Pressing her lips together tightly, she gracefully walked away. Logan watched her, noticing the men who were staring at her like starving coyotes looking at a freshly born lamb.

"You know, I've heard about you since I met Misty in college," William urbanely said, sipping at the sherry. "You sure did a number on her all those years ago. No one she's ever met since seems to last long. And yet, here you are."

Logan was irked by his cool, aloof manner. "I'm sure you tried."

"You misunderstand the nature of my and Misty's friendship. We recognized in each other two lost souls adrift in a world that we desperately wanted to fit into but weren't privileged or wealthy enough to gain access to. Well, not then, but times have certainly changed. We both have the wealth, but this is an enclave that will never treat us as equals and it's worse for Misty. She's the natural enemy of privileged white men. An intelligent, beautiful woman who's made it on her own, not inherited it." William sipped the last of his drink. "But I digress, Misty and I are friends and I think a great deal of her. I won't let her get hurt by you again. I might not be big and tough, but if I needed to, I could find a way to break you." Satisfied that he'd made his point, he looked down at his empty glass. "That's quite a good vintage."

The manicured man went up several notches in Logan's respect. He was glad that Misty had someone like William by her side while she'd swum these shark-infested waters. He was also fairly certain he didn't drink the same brand of beer as him. Looking across the room, Logan found her looking at him, and nerves he didn't even know he had calmed.

"William, Misty and I, well—" *What were they?* They weren't exactly friends, but she'd always been part of his life. Whenever they breathed the same air, she pulled him back to her like a magnet. And yet, he'd hurt her more than anyone else he'd ever cared about, and he did care about her. He glanced back to find William watching him perceptively. "I'll be leaving after the auction," Logan finished lamely.

The other man placed his glass on the tray of a passing waiter. "I think that would be for the best."

As the evening went by, Logan had never been so bored in his whole life, and he'd once watched paint dry on a dare from Bennett. He wasn't sure Misty enjoyed it all that much either. Her features had been set like they'd been sculptured from delicate porcelain. The Misty he knew lived with her emotions much closer to the surface. It had been a relief when she'd finally made their excuses and they'd headed for her penthouse. She'd immediately headed for her room to change and he'd gone straight to drink that other man's beer.

"Um, Logan, can you please do me a favor?"

He turned to find Misty several inches shorter now that she'd taken off her heels. "Yeah."

She turned to present her back to him. "I can't undo the zip, can you do it?" Logan's mouth went dry as he looked at the tiny zip that began at the nape of her neck. Fingers shaking ever so slightly, he set to work, barely breathing.

Enthralled, he watched as more creamy flesh was exposed as the crimson fabric parted.

"Thank you." She stepped away, breaking the spell. "After I've gotten changed, would you like to have a nightcap with me?"

He found himself drinking in the splendor of her coffee-colored eyes, framed by the handiwork of the makeup artist. Logan raised his drink. "I'm already ahead of you, but it would be nice to have some company." Misty gave him a quick smile and walked back to change, holding the back of her dress together.

When Misty returned, she quickly poured herself a wine and handed him a fresh can. "Won't he mind you giving away his beer?" Logan couldn't resist saying.

Misty looked at him blankly. "Who?"

"The guy whose beer I've been drinking. I assume you're getting it for someone. It doesn't really go with the rest of your alcohol collection." Even though he'd managed to keep his tone casual, jealousy lanced him.

She looked at him like he'd grown two heads. "I did get it for someone. You."

Now it was time for Logan to stare blankly at her. "Me?"

"I know you drink it and I wanted to make sure you were comfortable for your stay, so I asked Jeremy to stock up on it."

Her words made him happier than he had a right to feel. He turned to looked out the window to hide the smile that broke out at the thought that she didn't spend her nights up here sharing a nightcap with some other faceless man. Logan returned his gaze to her.

"Don't you get lonely here all alone? Heck, even I get lonely when I'm on the road."

Misty gave a decidedly unladylike snort. "I don't exactly

get the impression that you lack for company when you're on the road."

Logan laughed sheepishly, rubbing the back of his reddening neck. "Well, maybe not all the time." He grew serious. "I grew up surrounded by really, like, mind-blowingly talented people. Evelyn with her art. Colt was always going to be a champion. You were—heck, you still are the smartest person I've ever met. And well, Indie and Bennett, their talent was each other. But me? Me, I could barely read. The only talent I ever had was getting people to laugh at me. Trust me, that's a lonely way to live." He set his beer down on the coffee table and stood. "Thanks for the drink. I hope I did good tonight." Somehow it was more important than he had expected that she thought so, too. He left her sitting alone on the sofa before she could say otherwise. He didn't think he could bare it tonight if she did.

CHAPTER 14

$\mathcal{M}$isty had stayed on the sofa, frozen with emotions she didn't want to confront, long into the early hours of the morning. Even when she'd finally sought her bed, it had failed to provide a sanctuary against the tsunami that buffeted her. All her life, it had been easy to pigeonhole Logan. The jock. The best friend of her best friend's brother. And then as they got older, the guy who made her feel even when she desperately didn't want to. The man who haunted her dreams and broke her heart.

After a couple of hours of broken sleep, she gave up and padded drowsily toward the shower. Chora was arriving later today and, as a treat, she was taking her to the Ballet. Misty wasn't sure Logan would view it as much of a reward, but it was another good opportunity for the society ladies to see what they had the chance to win at the auction. There had been something about Logan last night, the mix of cowboy and fine tailoring that had made her breath catch every time she glimpsed him across the room. Maybe, if she was honest, it was why she was forcing him to dress up again tonight.

Deciding she wasn't going to waste any more time fixated on that rodeo clown—sorry, Rodeo Protection Athlete—she dressed for the office. Heaven knew there was always work to do, and she might as well get as much done as possible. Pausing on the way out the door, Misty quickly wrote a note for Logan. As if she could escape her thoughts as quickly as her penthouse, she strode out the door and away from the slumbering cowboy in the next room.

Inhaling her first cappuccino of the morning, she waited as her computer loaded up what felt like fifty million emails, her mind drifting as easily as the steam from her cardboard cup. It had actually been nice to have someone to come home with and discuss the day. Well, until it had gotten intense and Logan did what he always did in that situation and ran. Misty stared pensively at her computer screen. She'd never suspected the vulnerability he'd shown her last night. Sipping the creamy brew, she wondered if she should be relieved that, in a few days, he would be gone, and they would return to their usual status quo. Pondering, she found the relief lacking and a feeling of … emptiness? No, maybe she was just being overly sensitive that morning due to lack of sleep and stress. Surely the relief would come soon enough.

Finally, the screen came to life. *At last*. Pushing everything away, she immersed herself in the jumble of emails.

Several hours and cappuccinos later, she paused to draw breath. Emails had turned into proposals, and that had turned into delegating tasks. It was only the ringing of her phone that pulled her out of the vortex she'd willingly thrown herself into.

"Morning, Misty, I hope I didn't wake you," her brother greeted.

"Not likely. I've been at work for hours. What are you

doing up so early?" A quick glance revealed it was seven in the morning.

"Oh, is it? I had some things I needed to do," he replied vaguely. It sounded like he was really starting to get his life together. "I just wanted to let you know that I'm getting a ride up and back in one of the caterer's vans, but is it still okay to stay at your house?"

Pride flowed warmly through her. Brandon really had grown since he'd been on the inside. His determination to do the hard yards to become a chef was proof of that. "Of course you can. Hey, Brandon?"

"Yeah?"

"I know I was a little hesitant at first, but I'm a big enough girl to admit when I'm wrong, and man was I wrong. You're doing amazing, and I'm really proud of you." For a moment, Misty thought they'd been disconnected, the other end of the line remaining completely silent. "Are you still there?"

"Yeah." He cleared his throat. Obviously, he was feeling as choked up as she was. "That means a lot. I know I made a lot of mistakes, and I'm trying really hard to escape my past. You have no idea how much having you in my life is helping me."

She thought she could hear some muted voices in the background. It didn't sound like their parents. *Maybe he has a girlfriend?* It would make sense why he was starting his day so early. "I'll let you go. Just let me know when you're going to be there and I'll make sure that either myself is there or I let someone know to expect you if I'm not."

"Thanks, Misty."

She was still buzzing from her newfound relationship and trust in Brandon as she perused the clothing and accessories that had been curated for her to wear at the gala. She picked up a frothy creation. "What exactly do you call this color?" she queried the stylist.

"Ashes of rose."

She pursed her lips. "I'm not really sure I'm an ashes of rose kinda gal." She flicked past the white. Red, she'd already worn recently. Misty's hand hovered on the teal. It wasn't a color she usually felt drawn to.

"Ah, I see you've selected the Odessa." The stylist's voice was reverent. "It is a capsule piece."

"I'd like to try it on." Misty watched as the stylist took it from the rack. With deft movements, she was encapsulated in it, marveling at the way it caressed her skin as it draped over her body. The crossed-over bodice displayed enough flesh to show she was all woman without being tawdry. "I think this one will do nicely. Now what jewelry do you think?"

A sparkling set of chandelier diamond earrings, necklace and bracelet later, and she was wearing more than most people could afford to spend on several houses. "Breathtaking." The stylist pronounced, clapping her hands together in satisfaction.

Misty surveyed her image in the mirror, stroking the color of diamonds at her throat. In the center hung a pendant bigger than a robin's egg. "Can you please tell the jeweler that I will be purchasing these?"

"I'm sure he'll be pleased with your decision."

Misty smiled happily, an effervescent glow illuminating her like shopping and buying beautiful things always did. She rubbed her hands together with glee. "Now, let's talk shoes."

THERE WAS something about waking up to a note that always left a sour taste in a man's mouth. Sure, sometimes it was a good way to escape conversations a man didn't want to deal with, but that was when he was the one doing the leaving.

Muttering, Logan scrunched up the note and headed for the shower.

The blast of icy cold water sent prickles of goosebumps over his body. Taking about as much as he could, Logan stepped out, shaking the droplets from himself as he reached for the towel. Outside he could hear someone moving around. Wrapping the towel around his waist, he strode out, ready to give Misty a piece of his mind.

"What do you call leaving me a note telling me to dress up because I have to go to the Ballet tonight? Like I'm ever go to d—" Logan froze, looking at the honey blonde who had been in the process of opening a bottle of water, now staring at him open-mouthed. She was apparently unsure where to look, her eyes skittering from his face to his low-slung towel to his chest and then to the wall behind him. "Um, you're not Misty."

"Ah—" The blonde seemed to be having trouble speaking. "Ah," she repeated, swallowing. "Does Misty know you're walking around her penthouse like that greeting her guests?"

"Why, do you think she'd mind?" Logan couldn't resist asking, beating a retreat farther back to his bedroom.

"Um, well, it's not like she doesn't already have a nice enough view from here," came the laughing response. "Having more to look at would just be greedy."

Logan chuckled. He didn't know who this was, but he liked her. Pulling on a pair of jeans, he slipped a shirt over his head as he returned back to the living room. "I'm Logan Erikson, by the way."

Recognition flared across her face. He hadn't picked her as a rodeo fan, but they came in all shapes and sizes. "I remember you now. You were Colt's best man at his wedding." She held a hand to her chest. "I was there, too. I'm Chora. I run the Animals are Forever charity." Logan blinked at her blankly. "The one Misty's holding the gala for."

"Oh, right. I remember now."

Chora laughed off his lamely given response. "No, you don't. But I can't blame you. There were a lot of guests at that wedding."

Logan felt himself going red. "Well, I at least remember Misty mentioning that the auction at the gala was for a charity."

"And that's good enough for me. Now, which bedroom are you in?"

Logan could only stare at Chora in shock at her forthright proposal. "Um, you're a very attractive woman and I'm flattered, but I think it's best we don't mix business and pleasure."

His reaction seemed to amuse her as she brought her hand up to stifle her laughter. "I meant so I could put my stuff in the other guest bedroom. You know, the one you're not in," she said after managing to get herself under control. "You didn't think I meant with you, did you?"

"No, of course not."

"Well, good then, because I haven't had a chance to eat today and I'm famished, and I really don't want to eat alone. Do you know of any good places?"

"Not really, but I'm sure we can find one."

As he munched down on the burrito some time later, he found himself drawn in by Chora's passion. What she was doing with her charity, the commitment to being the change to the problem, was inspiring. He might have agreed to this auction to get a shiny gold sportscar and maybe to annoy Misty, but sitting here opposite the founder and hearing her stories, suddenly he was proud that he was helping a good cause.

"I admire what you're doing. How did you and Misty meet?" Logan asked around bites.

"I actually went to preschool with Misty. We were best

friends, and then we met Indie and Evelyn. We were just beginning to get close and, well, stuff happened, and my family moved to California."

"And now Misty supports your cause."

"It's not just me. All that art on the walls of Misty's apartment, she purchased them from artists who have donated to her various galas. A lot of them would still be struggling if she hadn't endorsed them." She cradled a cup of coffee in her hands.

"She lives very differently to how we grew up."

Chora laughed. "She lives a different life to most people. Doesn't change who she is."

"Well, not many people I know back home would be going to the Ballet tonight," he grumbled.

"I know, I'm so excited. I've been wanting to see *The Carnival of the Animals* for years now and just never got the time. I love the Ballet."

"Of course you do."

"And if I know Misty, if she wants you at the Ballet, you'll be at the Ballet." Chora smiled sweetly at him. "You might even enjoy it."

Logan gave her his best flat, unfriendly glare, which only set her to giggling more. He needed to get out of the city. The women here spend way too much time giggling at him.

He was still feeling sore about being bossed around when Misty came home. "You need to go put a suit on," she greeted him.

"Well, hi, Logan. How was your day?" He mimicked her voice. "It was fine, thank you for asking, Misty. And how was yours?"

The gorgeous object of his mocking narrowed her eyes at him, then glanced beside him to the giggling Chora. "Don't laugh. It only encourages him." Misty returned her gaze to his. "Fine," she huffed. "How was your day?"

"It was good, thank you. Chora and I had quite the enjoyable day. It started off unexpectedly, but I like to think she saw something she liked." Misty's brows shot up at his phrasing, suspiciously looking at the chortling Chora. "And how was yours?"

"It was fine. Now, please," Misty said, stressing the word, "go and put a suit on."

He couldn't resist. "Why?" he added with a faint smile of defiance.

"We're going to the Ballet," she ground out.

"No way. I'm not going."

"Yes. You. Are. It's part of the deal you signed up for."

Chora's eyes nervously darted between the two of them, and she stood suddenly. "I think I'll go and start getting ready." She quickly fled the battleground.

Misty continued to glare at him, and Logan mulishly set his jaw. The air crackled between them and he thought back to his earlier conversation and that shiny gold sportscar. "Fine, but I'm not going to like it."

She smiled sweetly at him. "That's fine, Logan, but you will be there." Muttering, he left her to her gloating.

It wasn't long before Logan had two sets of eyes inspecting him. "Oh my, we're going to raise a fortune for the charity." Chora breathed appreciatively.

Misty shot daggers at her friend before stepping forward to inspect him. This time he'd selected the black suit, but added a paisley shirt underneath and his large buckle from his freestyle bull fighter's championship, his faithful hat and trusty boots. She wanted a cowboy to auction, well, then he was going to dress like a darn cowboy.

He gave her a slow, lazy smile. "Well, am I going to make a lot of money at your gala?"

"I hope so. Otherwise this will have all been for nothing." Misty's words stung. "Come on, let's go."

Turns out, even with having a fancy private box at the theater and having women's hungry eyes following him as he made his way with Misty and Chora through the foyer, he was right. The Ballet was something that, if he never had to be put through that torture again, it would be too soon. To make it worse, Misty didn't even bother suggesting a nightcap when he'd suffered through it, simply suggesting everyone have a good night's sleep, and that tomorrow they'd leave for the Hamptons. *What the heck kind of suckful night was that?*

CHAPTER 15

*L*ogan wiggled on the smooth leather seat as he tried to get comfortable in the crowded town car, edging away from the shiny silver door handle that was digging in his side. Chora was sandwiched against him, Misty insisting on being the last person to enter the car. Dana had simply rolled her eyes at her boss and elected to sit in the front with the driver. Glumly, Logan looked out the window at the traffic that had ground to a halt. Trying to escape New York City on a Friday afternoon was harder than getting a pig out of a bog. *It was going to be one heck of a long drive.*

"I'm showing my age, but I remember when you could get into a helicopter on top of any skyscraper in New York City instead of having to make the drive to the airfield," Dana said conversationally from in front.

"Even driving to the airfield it's still better than sitting in traffic for hours on a Friday. There's no way I'm doing that when I can be in the Hamptons in under an hour," Misty said. Ten minutes later, they were on the tarmac and making their way to a sleek black helicopter.

"Have I told you how much I love your toys?" Chora eyed the helicopter appreciatively. "Like, really love."

"What can I say? It's one of the perks of the job." Misty smiled demurely, her eyes twinkling mischievously.

"The job of being a billionaire?" Logan stood to one side to let the ladies in before casting an appraising eye over the pilot who was doing his final checks. The silver hair could either be a cause for concern or confidence inspiring. A symbol of a man entering his dotage or a badge of experience. Logan chose to believe it was the latter.

Once the ladies had selected their seats, he was pleasantly surprised to discover a spare space directly opposite Misty and Dana, Chora being his neighbor. The white leather of the seat by now wasn't a surprise. He was beginning to suspect Misty might have something for the pale shade. The gleaming buckle on the harness was an indulgent gold, complementing the oak paneling nicely. It was opulent luxury, and every touch screamed Misty.

"Good afternoon, ladies and gentlemen, I'm Captain Wilson and I'm Misty's pilot for this poor old piece of junk." The target of the pilot's humor laughed under her breath. "If you'd like to take your seats and fasten your seatbelts, I'll have us up in the air and out of the city in no time." Taking note of the instructions, Logan settled back and prepared to have his first ever trip in a private helicopter.

As it rose gracefully into the air, he found himself among some of the most famous manmade landmarks in the world. Looking down, he could see the traffic that, only ten minutes before, they'd fought to break free from its tenacious grip snaking around the base of the buildings like sluggish rivers. It was a view that he knew only the privileged could afford, and one he was grateful he'd been afforded. Tearing his eyes away from the spectacular vista, he was bemused to see Dana and Misty oblivious to its majesty, furiously tapping away on laptops and murmuring between them. Chora's eyes gleamed appreciatively as she took in the view, clearly not immune to it the way the New Yorkers were.

"It's amazing what humans can do," she said.

Logan nodded, casting a look at Misty out of the corner of his eye. *It really was something.*

The jagged steel skyline fell away, leaving squares of urban sprawl until that too fell away and a carpet of green rolled out. As he felt them beginning to descend, he tried to spy which of the estates below could be Misty's. A large sprawling property caught his attention, dotted with several ponds and a broad expanse of beachfront.

"Is that one yours?'

Misty looked out the window and nodded. "Yep, home sweet home for the weekend."

"Darn, is that a basketball court beside the tennis courts?" It didn't seem fair. *Misty didn't even like basketball!*

"Yeah." She returned her attention to her screen, appearing to want to finalize things before landing.

Dana, several steps ahead of her boss, closed her computer. "That's not all. It's quite the estate, and Misty had to outbid several other interested parties to purchase it. Currently it's the most expensive property to have ever been sold in the Hamptons."

"What, is the bathroom made out of gold?" Logan couldn't resist asking, trying to shrug off the intimidation he felt that Misty had achieved all this on her own merit. He might be intimidated, but he sure as heck was proud of her, too.

"Not any of the twelve bathrooms I've seen."

"I guess there won't be any queues for one while we're there." He paused. "That's a lot of bathrooms to clean."

"And the estate has a fulltime housekeeper as well as a groundsman. I suggested Misty get a butler, but she declined." Dana shook her head at her boss, mock disappointment painted all over her face.

Misty closed her computer, laughing. "You only wanted one so you could say that the butler did it every time something went missing."

"Yes, and you went and squashed my dream like a bug."

"I don't need a butler," Misty said firmly.

"Your place looks huge." Chora stared out the window, bracing for landing.

The jolt was surprisingly smooth, the pilot obviously knowing what he was doing. "It's a forty-two-acre estate with twelve bedrooms,"

"Don't forget the twelve bathrooms," Logan interrupted Dana to add.

"And twelve bathrooms. The main house is a little over twenty thousand square feet, that's not including the guesthouse. It also has a twenty-foot pool, a greenhouse, helipad, tennis courts, basketball courts, hot tub, and room for at least six cars." Dana drew breath, smiling as the pilot opened the helicopter door for them.

Logan gave a low whistle as he set foot on terra firma. "Do you ever get lost?"

Misty pushed some stray strands of hair from her face, whipped up by a briny smelling breeze. "Not really. I spend most of my time on my beach."

Chora looked over her shoulder. "That beach is yours, too?"

Misty had the grace to look slightly embarrassed by the riches of her good fortune. "Only about a quarter of a mile."

"Only about a quarter of a mile," Logan spluttered, incredulous at her admission. "Darn, gal, why would you ever leave?" *Why hadn't she ever mentioned this?* Heck, he was beginning to discover that there were a lot of things Misty had never bragged about. He'd always suspected she was out of his league or would be one day, but seeing this, he realized they weren't even on the same continent.

"Well, in summer I spend every weekend that I'm not visiting Evelyn or in Europe here." Misty gestured for them to follow her. "But then again, most people who can afford to flee New York in summer do. Now, if you come with me, I'll show you where you'll be staying." Head held high, she led the way across the manicured lawn and into her palatial domain.

IT WAS like walking into a construction site of flowers, caterers, marquees and madly rushing staff. Having handed her guests into the capable hands of her housekeeper, she surveyed the scope of work that still needed to be completed. Misty had gathered a crack team, but she still felt the familiar jitters that something would go wrong and it wouldn't be perfect. In the distance she could see her brother setting up around the caterer's area, the vans circled liked something from the wild west. Brandon briefly glanced up, but didn't return her wave. Maybe he didn't see her. She'd been informed by Mrs Bronson that he'd been in the house only long enough to select a bedroom and stow his gear before returning to the frontlines again.

"Wow, I've seen less people at a national rodeo."

Misty jumped at Logan's voice. She wondered if he'd seen her trying to get Brandon's attention. *I probably looked like an idiot, jumping around waving.* Logan still irritated her more than anyone else she'd ever met, but lately it didn't have the sting it used to. *Maybe we're growing up.*

"It possibly costs more."

He tugged at the brim of his hat. *Good Lord, was there anything as gorgeous as a man in a Stetson and cowboy boots?* "I reckon I believe that. Now, I left Dana and Chora with their heads together going over last-minute details or something. Is there anything I can help you with?"

"You can keep me company if you like," she blurted, caught off guard by this man she didn't know whether to hate or love.

"Heck, that doesn't sound like work at all."

His irresistibly devastating smile made Misty lose her train of thought, a smile unconsciously tugging at her lips in reply. "You say that now. You won't by the time we finish."

Logan, a spark of something indecipherable gleaming in his eyes, held out his arm to her. "Lead the way, boss lady."

Feeling ever so slightly giddy, she linked her arm with his. The way Logan looked at her made her heart beat in a way that only he'd ever been able to do. "I like it when you call me boss."

He leaned in close, his warm breath in her ear. "I thought you would." A dizzying current of emotions dissolved her resolve. Maybe she didn't hate him after all.

Long into the afternoon and evening, he remained at her side, giving opinions on everything from the placement of floral arrangements to helping move chairs. His constant companionship had made a stressful afternoon fly by. Brandon had at last returned to the house, bearing food sent up by the caterers. If he'd seemed quiet and standoffish, Misty blamed it on a day that was just as long and stressful as her own. She made a mental note to check in and see how he was going tomorrow with his employers. Watching her friends' eyes begin to droop, Misty had sent everyone to bed. Tomorrow everyone needed to shine, and she didn't need her friends to be dull from lack of sleep.

Soon she would seek her own bed, but first Misty needed to check the lighting of the marquee. Standing at the end of her pool, she could glimpse it, twinkling like a fairy castle at the bottom of the garden. Misty caught a glimpse of her reflection. She'd taken her hair down to ease the beginning of a headache and now the lights glinted off it as it hung loose around her shoulders. The woman staring back at her looked younger, her eyes gleaming with an energy that flowed from her soul.

"You look like a fairy princess." Logan's low voice felt intimate as it drifted to her.

Misty gazed up to find him staring at her, his eyes filled with a curious deep longing. A soft laugh escaped her pent-up breath. "Hardly."

"You're right." He came closer, gently tucking a strand of hair behind her ear. "A fairy queen." Misty felt like her heart had dropped from her chest. The only movement she was capable of was trying to remember to breathe. "Will there be dancing tomorrow?"

"Yes, why?"

He gently pulled her toward him and wrapped his arms low around her waist. "I thought I might ask for a dance, but now I'm not so sure." Logan's words cut deep. Stiffly, she tried to pull back, but his strong arms held her rigid body firm. "Seeing you standing here under the moonlight, a man would be mad not to ask now. Misty, will you dance with me?"

Her heartbeat skyrocketed as he retrieved her limp hand and raised it to his lips, pressing a kiss to the palm of her hand before closing her fingers around it. "When was the last time you danced?" A tremor shook Misty's voice.

"I do it all the time." Wounded, her eyes flew to his, imagining all the women he'd danced with. "The bulls make sure I never step on their toes when we dance." Logan pulled her in close to his hard, strong body and began to sway as he hummed softly.

Misty colored, feeling silly. "I haven't danced in a long

time."

"I know, and you need to do it more. While we're at it, you need to wear your hair down more. I get it, not at work, but don't get old and hard before your time." They continued to sway, Misty scarcely breathing, terrified she'd break this spell that wrapped around them. "Misty, I'm sorry about Christmas and being a jerk in high school and pretty much every time we spend more than five minutes together."

"I already forgave you when you apologized last time."

"Yeah, but I'm not so sure I really meant it then. This time it's a proper apology."

Misty gave a light laugh. "At least you're honest, I guess. I forgive you. Again."

A chuckle rumbled in his chest. "Good. I can sleep tonight."

"Hey, Logan?"

"Yeah?"

"I just wanted to say you're just as talented as the rest of us, but in your own way."

"This sounds awfully like a participation award speech."

"What you do takes skill and guts. And back in school, you weren't stupid. You had dyslexia. It wasn't your fault that no one figured it out till you were almost grown." The touch of his hand was almost unbearable in its tenderness as it gently touched her face. Misty's heart took a perilous leap as he gazed at her, slowly lowering his mouth to hers. The touch of his lips sent shockwaves through her entire body, and for a moment, she lost herself in it.

Misty pulled back, freeing herself from his embrace and emotions she didn't want to feel. As she disappeared through the night back to the house, she heard Logan call her name, but she didn't look back, knowing he would still be standing there beside the reflections in the pool. She might forgive him, but she wasn't ready to get her heart broken again.

CHAPTER 16

*L*ying in bed last night, Misty's mind had burned with the memory of Logan's kiss. How had she let herself get sucked back into the vortex that was Logan Erikson? She'd been caught in his wake before and she wasn't stupid enough to think it would end any other way this time. Didn't stop a girl from wishing.

Determined to act like it hadn't happened had proven to be easier than she'd thought when she'd got up that morning. Brandon was the only person moving around, the others apparently catching up on their beauty sleep.

"How did yesterday go?" Misty asked quietly, padding into the kitchen on slippered feet. "You didn't really say much last night."

Brandon jerked. Recovering, he continued to butter his toast. The rough drag of the knife against bread was loud in the stillness of the room. "It was pretty hectic." His smile wasn't quite enough to chase the shadows under his eyes away. "It felt good to be doing something useful. You know —" The knife stilled its ceaseless movement. Brandon's expression, the way he looked at her, it was like he wanted her to really understand. "I've made a lot of mistakes and I still do, but I'm trying. I'm doing the best I can, even if it sometimes feels like I'm still paying for my past."

Misty looked down as she poured her cup of coffee, guilt wrapping around her as surely as the steam rose from her brew. "Brandon, I'm really sorry if I've done anything to make you feel like that."

Brandon set down the butter knife. "You haven't done anything but give me more forgiveness than I deserve. I'm going to make it up to you, all the broken trust and times I wasn't there for you as a big brother looking out for you."

Tears stung her eyes as she sniffed. "I love you, Brandon, and I'm proud you're my brother."

Brandon swallowed. With two quick steps, he wrapped her up in a bear hug. "You have no idea how much that means to me, hearing you say it. I love you too, never forget that." Just as quickly as he hugged her, he was stepping back. Grabbing his toast from the plate, he headed for the door. "I better not be late for work. I hear the lady hosting this gala can be a real dragon," he threw over his shoulder as he disappeared from sight.

Misty chuckled. *Man, it was good having Brandon back in her life.* Taking her coffee, she headed back to her room. A shower would be good while she waited for the caffeine to hit her system, and then she was going to bring her A-game to all the finishing touches that still needed to be done. Maybe by then the rest of her guests might even be awake. Although she wasn't really sure if she was ready to face Logan again, not with the weight of the kiss between them.

With a lot of effort and a little luck, it turned out it was surprisingly easy to avoid a cowboy when setting up a gala if you really wanted to. As the day wore on, every time Logan so much as glanced in her direction and tried to get her alone, she suddenly found somewhere else she needed to be or a person she urgently needed to speak with. It had been a relief when the stylist had arrived with makeup and hair artists in tow to help her, Chora and Dana get ready.

"I love that dress on you," complimented Chora from where she was seated, rollers sitting atop her head.

Misty gave a slow twirl, grinning happily at the way it whispered as she moved. "Me too." She stopped, waiting patiently as the stylist came over and began to fasten her necklace. Looking at her reflection, Misty thought the diamonds were worth every last penny she'd paid for them. "I'm going to leave you ladies in capable hands and make sure there aren't any last-minute disasters that need averting."

"Call me if there are," Dana murmured, her eyes closed as the makeup artist applied color to her eyes.

Misty waved her PA's suggestion aside. "Enjoy the pampering. Once you leave the tranquility of here, it's going to be all hands on deck."

"And I guess there's a certain cowboy you need to see, you know, to make sure he's ready to shake his money maker," Dana called after her.

Chora snorted. "I'm not sure Logan knows that's what's expected of him. Anyway, I think the ladies will be throwing money at him just for giving them that look. You know the one. Eyes all sultry and that smile."

"Okay, Chora, we get the idea." Misty didn't like the thought of Logan looking like that at just anyone. "And I guess you're right. I'll see if Logan is ready." A tingle settled in her stomach, intensifying as she got closer to his door. Her mouth dry, she knocked.

"Who is it?" Logan's drawl sounded from inside.

"Housekeeping," she replied in a falsetto.

He opened the door and leaned indolently against the frame, devilishly handsome. His gaze roved lazily, taking in her appearance. "You look like no housekeeping I've ever seen."

Misty's heart beat faster as she drank in the sight of him. His broad shoulders filled the charcoal shirt he wore, his stance emphasizing the strength of his thighs and slimness of his hips. Good Lord, he was hot. Had anyone else ever made her feel the way he did?

Logan grinned at her, his teeth white against his tanned skin. "Cat got your tongue?"

"No, I was just trying to see you how the ladies will tonight." *Liar. I don't ever want anyone looking at him like I do, like he's mine.* Misty swallowed, she really needed to get a grip. He fidgeted with his sleeve. It was only then that she noticed that one cuff had been buttoned and the other dangled undone. "Here, let me help you with that." Smiling at her, a warmth smoldering in his eyes, Logan held it out to her. The minute she touched him, she knew she'd made a mistake, a familiar shiver of awareness rippling through her. "There, done." She smiled brightly up at him.

Logan's hands slipped up her arms, bringing her closer. "Have you been avoiding me?"

Misty dropped her gaze, dwelling on his beautiful mouth. "No, I just had a lot to do."

"Good, I thought maybe you regretted last night." He was so close she could smell the toothpaste on his breath. "Because I don't."

His hand crept to the back of her neck, his touch almost unbearable in its yearning tenderness. And then he was kissing her, filling her senses. But somehow time moved too fast, and Misty bit down on a frustrated whimper when he pulled away.

"I'm sorry."

Her heart sunk at his words. "For kissing me?"

Logan gave a low laugh. "No, I've never regretted that."

He gently touched her face. "You look so beautiful and perfect and, well"—he gave another little laugh—"your lipstick isn't perfect anymore."

"Oh." Misty held a trembling hand to her lips. "I should probably go fix that."

"Ms Monroe," the housekeeper called. "Your other guest has arrived."

"There's no need to announce me, it's not like she's the queen or something." William sidestepped the woman, raising an eyebrow at the close proximity of the pair in front of him. "I see I've arrived just in time."

Misty told herself she was a grown woman, but still blushed under his words. "Aren't you cutting it a little fine? I thought you were meant to be here hours ago." She made her way over to him, fighting the pull to return to Logan's arms.

"Well, someone had to deal with the dramas you left me with." William looked over her shoulder. "Hello, Logan." Something seemed to pass between them, but Misty wasn't sure what.

"Hello, William."

"You're in your usual room, if you want to freshen up and change. I'll go touch up my makeup. The others should be ready soon too, and then we can all head over to the marquee. Our guests should be arriving in half an hour."

And then it wouldn't be long before she was giving Logan to the highest bidder.

LOGAN CLOSED the door on the sight of William walking away with Misty, heartily wanting to throttle the man. If last night's kiss had set his blood on fire, then today Misty had melted his very bones. Maybe it was a good thing that, by the end of the weekend, he'd be flying home to Texas, away from that gorgeous temptress, before he lost control over his wayward heart. If that happened, he knew in his soul that he'd never be able to leave, even if she didn't want him.

That's the way it was with Misty. She was dangerous. One taste was never enough. Heck, it was why he always left first before he could get addicted. He'd been scared of loving that gal since he was sixteen, but that didn't mean he hadn't. She was no longer the naïve young girl she'd been, untested by life. Logan raked his fingers through his hair before slamming his hat into place. Heck, he hadn't come out without a few scars of his own. But she made him feel alive, and more than that, she made him want to grow old with her. Knowing there wasn't a happy ever after on the cards for them, he gave himself one final glance in the mirror and stalked to the door. *I need a drink.*

I should have had more to drink, Logan thought later, twitching the curtain closed and wiping his sweaty palms on his pants. It seemed like a lifetime ago that he'd agreed to the auction when Colt had dangled his shiny gold sportscar in front of him. Back then it had seemed like no big deal. Heck, he was used to performing in front of crowds—and dealing with raging bovines to boot. Standing here now, hearing Misty auction off a probably priceless vase, he began to quickly consider how much time remained to formulate an escape.

"Feeling nervous?" Chora appeared and handed him a bottle of water.

"Petrified."

"Really? I'd think this would be a walk in the park for a guy like you."

"Bulls I can handle, but cougars scare me." Logan lifted his hat slightly to wipe at his brow.

"Better get it over with then, like a band aid." Chora took the bottle from him, and with a strength that was at odds with her slight body, pushed him through the curtain and onto the stage. Blinking at the bright lights, Logan found himself staring at a sea of gaping faces.

Seeing Misty give a sharp jerk of her head, he ambled over. "The next item is a rare prize. A genuine cowboy from Texas."

"Five hundred," came from the crowd.

"Wow, and we're off to a good start." Misty began to warm to her subject. "Logan is the nation's best Rodeo Protection Athlete, having won the national championship."

"One thousand." Logan was startled to see a white-haired woman, immaculate in black and pearls, and looking to not see eighty again bid.

"Ladies, believe me when I tell you that a Texas cowboy has been raised right and knows how to treat a woman." Misty gave him a sideways glance, her gaze intent.

"Ten thousand."

"Now we're starting to get somewhere. I'm sure you'll all agree that such a gorgeous cowboy is worth more than that." Misty fanned herself with her notes. "This is one hot man."

"Fifteen thousand."

"Twenty thousand." The old lady had re-entered the bidding. The way she was looking at him wasn't entirely grandmotherly. Apprehension trickled down his spine. His mom had never taught him what to do in a situation like this.

"He loves to dance." There was an odd note to Misty's voice. Logan peered at her. Something was going on with her, but he wasn't sure what.

"Fifty thousand." A new voice entered the bidding, Logan found himself staring at a mature blonde, waving her number baton languidly in the air. She looked at him like a starving kid did cake and yet at the same time coolly detached. Suddenly Grandma bidding didn't seem so bad.

"But I can't guarantee the condition he'll return in." Laughter greeted her statement.

Misty's mouth worked as she glared narrow-eyed at the other woman. Logan had seen that look before and it always came seconds before the fireworks. "Sixty thousand." Logan stared at her. *What was she doing?*

The blonde's mouth stretched into an unflattering line, quite a marvel, given the rest of her face didn't change expression. "Seventy."

"Eighty." Misty's nostrils flared as the assembled guests' gazes swung back to their host like spectators at a tennis match.

"Two hundred thousand dollars." There was a note of triumph in the blonde's voice. Misty's mouth worked, but no sound came forth.

"And sold," Chora declared walking onto stage.

"You make sure he's well rested when I come to collect him," the blonde said smugly, wrapping her red-taloned hand around the stem of a champagne glass. "I wouldn't want him to disappoint after what I just paid for him."

Her expression bordered on contempt. "I'll remind you that you only purchased the right to go on a date with him." Misty's voice was icy, at odds with the heat blazing in her eyes.

"Well, I guess that's up to him." Misty stiffened at the other woman's smug retort. Logan was surprised she didn't snap a tooth from the way her jaw was furiously working.

"I believe that concludes the auction part of tonight's gala," Chora smoothly interjected, shooting Misty a puzzled glance. "We'd like to thank everyone for their kind donations. If my calculations are correct—and believe me, there's a reason I pay someone to do the books for the charity— we've raised over two million dollars tonight. Put your hands together."

To the polite applause of the crowd, Chora dragged Misty and Logan off the stage. "That was a great idea, Misty."

Misty blinked at her friend. "What do you mean?"

"Bidding yourself to bump the bid up. No way did I think Logan would raise that much money." Chora smiled apologetically at him. "No offense, Logan."

"None taken, just happy to do my small part for a great cause." His mind was struggling to piece together the events that had just unfolded.

"I'm just glad it worked." Misty's words didn't ring true to Logan, and the look she returned was closed. "Now, if you'll excuse me, I should go and mingle." Back ramrod straight, she briskly walked away.

"If I didn't know better, I'd think she was jealous," Chora marveled as if she'd just seen a fire-breathing Care Bear in the flesh. "And she never gets jealous. Mad, irritated, yes. Jealous, no."

"Yeah, well, I know her better, and she isn't jealous. Not of me going on a date." But Logan could help wondering if maybe it was true. Or was that just wishful thinking?

CHAPTER 17

*D*amn Logan, always making me act the fool. After her performance on stage, Misty had gone into full-blown damage control, laughingly accepting people's admiration for her ploy to drive up bidding. Thinking about it this morning still made her want to bury her head under the pillow and pretend it was all just a bad dream. *No, the bad dream was Lilian Westminster getting her taloned hands on Logan.* The thought was enough to make her see as red as the blonde socialite's claws. *And Logan, well, he just ate it up.*

A knock on the door made her pull the covers up. "Who is it?"

"Just me." A pause. "Brandon," he clarified. "I'm about to leave and I wanted to say goodbye."

Misty sat up in bed. "You can come in." Her brother entered, giving her room a surreptitious glance. "So, how was it? Do you still want to be a chef? I know doing the grunt work isn't quite the same."

"More than anything, it's what I want to do. I don't ever want to go back to how I was." He spoke with a quiet, almost desperate firmness. "They asked if I want to work for them permanently, and they even mentioned that after I prove myself, they'll help me go to culinary school. Thanks for making it happen for me."

Misty's heart sang with happiness at the gleam of pride on her brother's face. "I helped you with the contact. You got the rest of it by working hard and making a good impression." She scrunched her face. "Will it be a go with your parole officer if you move here?"

Brandon shrugged. "I hope so. I mean, it's a steady job, which is something I don't have in Florida. I guess if I can show them that I have that and somewhere to live, it'll work out."

"You can live with me." It would be nice to have him around, the thought surprising in how much she liked the idea.

"Well, I guess we can talk about that later." Brandon looked away, swallowing. Misty got the distinct impression there was more he wanted to say. Looking back at her, odd shadows danced in the depths of his eyes. "Anyway, I need to get going if I'm going to get a ride. You're leaving today, aren't you?"

"Yeah." *It's not like she was going to hang around and hear all about Logan's date.* "Logan leaves tomorrow morning, but tonight he'll be out."

Brandon nodded. "Okay, maybe we can catch up sometime. If you want."

"Of course I want to catch up with my big brother. Now, come here and give me a hug."

There was a desperation to the way he pulled her in and squeezed as if he never wanted to let go. Misty had forgiven him for the past. She prayed he would do the same for himself. "Okay, have a safe drive. I love you."

"I love you too, Misty." Brandon waved awkwardly and left.

Misty looked indecisively at her bed. Maybe she could just stay here until it was time to go. Her phone began to vibrate on her nightstand, Evelyn's name flashing on the screen. Honestly, she was amazed her friend had waited until the sun rose to find out what had happened last night.

"Two hundred thousand," Misty answered the phone with.

"What?"

"Two hundred thousand dollars. That's what some frozen blonde paid to have a date with Logan."

"That's great! I knew you would raise lots of money, but that's a lot more than I'd thought." Evelyn sounded disgustingly chuffed with herself. "And to think Logan wasn't going to do it until Colt bribed him with a sportscar."

Ice settled in the pit of Misty's stomach. Logan had never wanted to spend time with her at all. It had just been so he could get some stupid car. "Oh, really?" Her voice was frigid.

"You didn't know, did you?"

"I'm an idiot. I should have known better." *The whole time, he was just playing her.* A crushing sense of loss knocked the happiness from her very being.

"Okay, Misty, I think it's time you tell me exactly what's been going on, and you can start with when you and Logan started avoiding each other." The ring of command in Evelyn's voice was enough to brook no refusal.

As the words spilled from her, all her confusion and heartbreak welded together into a knot around her soul. "And then I don't know what happened, but something snapped, and I didn't want someone to win the date with him. I wanted be the one going." Misty finished miserably.

"So, are you going to admit it?" Evelyn asked sympathetically.

"Admit what? That I've been an idiot?" *That had to be the understatement of the year.*

"Well, yes, but that's not what I had in mind. That you're in love with him."

A tumble of confused thoughts and emotions assailed her. "I'm not in love with him. I mean, I don't think so."

"Misty, you've had it bad for him for years. Colt says you're the only gal Logan's ever kept coming back to. Maybe it's both of your prides that's stopping you from staying together." Misty rocked back. Could what Evelyn said be true? Did Logan care about her, too?

She was going to find out—and before that darn date tonight, too. "Evelyn, I have to go."

"Let me know what happens."

"Who says anything's going to happen?"

"Oh, please. Just call me afterwards with all the juicy details."

"Thanks, Evelyn." Misty hung up the phone. First, she needed to see her friends off. There was no way she was leaving now. Not before she had a chance to find out how Logan really felt.

Logan risked a glance at Misty as they waved William, Chora and Dana off, watching as the pilot seemed to linger a little longer assisting the PA. Maybe Dana's luck was about to change. Misty hadn't said much to him, busy with her friends' departure, but now there was nothing but a big empty house, a housekeeper and them. He wasn't really sure what mood she was in after last night, and he couldn't quite read her expression. Genuine terror snaked in his stomach at what could happen next.

"Do you want to go for a swim?" Misty asked, turning to head back to the house.

"Isn't it a bit cold? He tugged his denim jacket about him

for emphasis, the move redundant since the thought of her in a swimsuit was warming him up nicely.

"The pool's heated." She gave him a saucy little smile. "Or are you scared?"

"Scared? Of what?" Cold water? Nope. Her? Definitely. Logan was feeling twitchier than a spring bull.

"I'll find out soon enough. I'm going to get changed, and I guess I'll either see you or won't at the pool." Her voice held a silky challenge as she sent him a final look, something lurking in the depths of her dark eyes, just out of reach. And then with her hips swaying, she walked away.

Logan took a steadying breath. *You're not some randy sixteen-year-old boy.* Getting himself firmly under control, he followed behind her at as much of a sedate pace as he could manage. That didn't stop him breaking several speed records while changing into his swimming trunks. He'd bought them on the shopping trip with Dana when he'd seen them marked down, never expecting to use them so soon.

He made it to the pool just as she stepped out of her slippers and shed her fluffy robe. Logan's mouth went bone dry at the sight of her lithe form diving into the steaming water. Somehow he'd lost the power to breathe. Quickly divesting himself of his own outerwear, he joined her in taking the plunge. As he surfaced, Logan had to admit it was the perfect temperature. Speaking of perfect, his gaze sought Misty.

"You can stop looking at me like that." The devilish gleam in her eyes declared otherwise.

"I think you enjoy it." He smiled smugly at her. "I know you enjoy kissing me."

Misty's face, already flushed from the heat of the water, deepened in color. "We've kissed twice … this year," she finished lamely.

"It's been a good year," he agreed, smirking at her. "I think it's the longest we've gone without you wanting to kill me."

"Or you making me feel that way," she tartly replied, lifting that gorgeous chin of hers.

Logan knew he was going to regret this, but he desperately needed to know. "Do you want to talk about last night?"

"Oh, here we go. You want to gloat about how much money you raised." Misty began to paddle away. Logan reached out, taking hold of her leg and pulling her back to him, causing her to splash while trying to free herself. "Let me go, Logan."

"Not this time." Never again if he had anything to say about it. "I can do this all day."

"No, you can't, you have a date to go on," she bit out.

"A date that you arranged for me, remember? You wanted my help to raise money at your gala. Are you mad at me because I'm going on this date?" Did she actually bid on him for herself? Logan's heart lurched hopefully. Maybe she did care after all.

"No, I bid because I didn't want to see you with Lilian Westminster." Misty squirmed free to glare at him. "She's a known maneater. I mean, she's been married five times!" she declared hotly.

"And you're worried I can't look after myself, like she'll trick me into marrying her after one date?"

"Hardly. Anyway, I know the real reason why you decided to help me."

"Yeah?"

"Yeah." Bitterness laced the word. "Because Colt offered you some fancy sportscar and then suddenly you had time for me again." Her shoulders drooped. "I'm so sick of these games. It's tiring. I think I'm immune to you, and you pull me back in, only to hurt me and run away."

"It started with Colt offering me that car, but nothing I did here was planned. I'm as powerless to resist this as you are. Have you ever wondered why we keep finding our way back to each other?" His hand found the small of her back in the water and pulled her closer, lifting her chin with the other. "I'm not running away this time."

Misty's lashes were black spikes against her cheeks as she dropped her gaze. "Yeah, but I am." A world of hurt and regret swam in her dark eyes as she lifted them to meet his. "Well, maybe this time you can feel what it's like to be the one left behind."

Her words slammed into Logan like a freight train, the shock of them causing his hand to drop. "Misty, you don't mean that. What we have—" He swallowed. How did he even describe what it was? "It's special."

She pushed away from him, swimming to the edge of the water. Gracefully pulling herself out, Misty wrapped the fluffy robe around her like armor. "Why is this time any different from the others? Each of those times, I went into it leading with my heart. This time, I'm protecting it." There was a tremor to her voice as she fought her emotions. "I hope you have a good date with Lilian."

Heart shattered, all Logan could do was watch her walk away, knowing he deserved her mistrust, but dang if it didn't still hurt. *This time was different*, his heart screamed into the emptiness she left behind as he slowly sunk beneath the silent water to ease his misery.

CHAPTER 18

Misty trailed a finger along the back of the pool lounge, restless in the quiet of the inky night, bringing her wineglass to her lips. The solitude was something she normally yearned for, a respite for her fried nerves from the stress of her professional life. It was the closest she felt to home outside of Colt and Evelyn's ranch. Tonight, with Logan gone on his date, it just felt lonely. The steam from the pool rose into the still night, her earlier words returning to haunt her. It had been wounded pride that had made her reject him. She loved him, after all.

But what would it be like to have Logan fully in her life, committed to them? Misty tried to picture him living in Manhattan with her and the thought of him drifting about her penthouse doing lunch with the ladies was too ludicrous to entertain. Jeremy would probably love it. Maybe he could live here in the Hamptons and she could come up on the weekends. It occurred to her that she was imagining him as a househusband, and Logan just wasn't the sort of guy to sit around looking handsome and waiting for her.

Maybe she could buy a ranch in Texas for them. How

cool would it be to have Evelyn and Colt as neighbors? Their kids could grow up together. She pictured two little dark-haired best friends, Hope bossing them around. *Whoa, slow down, girl.* The visions dancing in her head called to her, tantalizing a future that, no matter how appealing, didn't matter. She'd ended it and she'd been right to do it, too. Why then did her heart beg her to reconsider?

A rustle in the bushes gave her a start. "Henry?" she called to the groundsman. "Is that you?" Alarm slammed into Misty, her heart beating painfully in her chest as she struggled to think of a reason why he would still be here. Even her house-keeper had gone out to dinner for her night off. "Whoever you are, you need to show yourself or I'm calling the police." She fumbled in her pocket for her phone, realizing she'd left it inside when she'd poured herself the wine. "I mean it." Even she could hear the tremor that made a mockery of her bravado.

The branches twitched and Misty, having always heard about the fight or flight response, realized there was a third response. Freezing, horrifying paralyzation. Brandon emerged from the shrubbery. Regardless of his familiar face, her stomach still clenched tightly.

"Sorry, Misty."

"What are you doing here?" she demanded. "You nearly gave me a heart attack."

Brandon still didn't step forward into the light. "I'm sorry," he repeated. "You weren't meant to be here. Why aren't you in Manhattan with the others?"

"Because I changed my mind. I don't really think it's any of your business if I stayed or not." Anxiety coursed through her. Something was very wrong here. The tingle of alarm she'd felt earlier now returned with force, like she'd grabbed hold of an electric fence.

"Yeah, but it's ours," a gravelly voice sneered as another

two shapes materialized in the darkness behind Brandon. It was a voice that didn't belong here on her estate, not when she was alone. Real fear gripped her.

"Brandon, what's going on?" It felt like her words were coming from far away.

"I'm sorry. I tried to make things better, but they pull you back in. Once they have a hold over you, you can't escape, no matter how much you want to."

Misty's body shook off the paralysis and she fled, terror making her nimble across the tiles as the faceless men burst through the shadows after her. Terror forced all conscious thought from her mind, her body fueled by adrenaline and the need to escape.

WAS it possible that his watch wasn't working? Maybe the battery was going flat.

Crimson nails dug unpleasantly into his arm. "I've never touched a real-life cowboy before. Are you as rugged all over as you appear?"

"Ma'am, that's for me to know."

"And for me to find out?" Lilian purred seductively. At least, that's what Logan thought she was striving for. It was having the opposite effect on him.

"I don't believe that was in my contract for tonight." The way she kept clawing at him, he was beginning to hold grave concerns for the fancy shirt Misty had paid a small fortune for.

"Maybe we should see where the night leads." Lilian coyly trailed her fingers up his arm, leaving a divot behind in the fabric. It was going to be a small miracle if it wasn't torn to shreds by the end of the night.

Firmly, he removed her hand from his arm. "I'm pretty

sure I know how this evening is going to end. You going home to your bed and me going home to mine. Alone," he added for emphasis.

Thoughts of Misty waiting at home for him whispered in his mind. Logan had left her, stubborn pert little nose up in the air and acting like she was perfectly all right with him leaving on a date with another woman. But Misty didn't share. Never had and never would. And he sure as heck didn't want her to. It was time he told her exactly how their future was going to be—the two of them, maybe a couple of mini-mes, and that was that. Glancing at his watch, he bit back a frustrated sigh.

"Now, tell me how you ended up having to pay for a date."

"Well, it all began after my fifth husband died on our wedding night." Lilian held her hand to her chest. "The poor dear just wasn't up to it."

Logan knew how he felt.

HER BREATH CAME IN SHORT, ragged gasps. Misty screamed as she felt her leg get taken out from underneath her and she toppled to the ground, the last of the air knocked from her lungs. Stunned, she could only lay limp as she was hauled back to her feet. Panic like she'd never known before welled in her throat. Sucking in oxygen, she began to scream for help, struggling with every ounce of her strength. Blindly, she flailed against the man who held her. If she was going to die, she wasn't going to make it easy for them.

Misty gasped at the shock of being slapped, staring at the shorter of the men, panting in terror. "Shut up." It was the one who had spoken before. "Brandon, control your sister, or I will." His voice was absolutely emotionless, and it chilled her to her core.

Brandon shoved the man holding Misty out of the way and took a grip on her arm. "Misty, I swear if you just do what he tells you, everything's going to be okay. We're going to be okay."

Loathing filled her as she looked at him. "I trusted you."

"I know, and I never meant for it to get to this." Brandon looked like he was about to be sick.

"What a touching scene." The leader clapped his hands together sarcastically. "Now, be a good girl and show us where you keep the expensive stuff."

Stiffly, she led them into the house and watched as they ransacked it, knocking over antique vases and ripping artwork from the walls. The leader let out a string of curses, rounding on Brandon. "I thought you said she had stuff worth taking! It was the only reason I didn't break your legs when you didn't have the money you owed me."

"But this is good stuff," Brandon protested. "It's worth a lot of money."

"Yeah, but we have to sell it first, and stuff like that, it's hard to fence." He leaned in close to Misty. She shuddered away from the onslaught of his fetid breath. "Now, little girl, where's your safe? Your jewelry?" She swallowed, nodding her chin toward her bedroom. "There better be something worthwhile in there or it won't just be your brother who's going to get hurt."

She led the way to her walk-in closet, past her clothes to reveal the hidden safe. Her thumb shook as she held it up to the touchpad. When it clicked open, Misty stepped back to reveal the contents inside. It sickened her to watch them roughly handle the diamond jewels that, less than twenty-four hours earlier, had filled her with such pleasure.

"These are more like it. Now, a pretty little thing like you, you'd have lots of money easy to access. Where are your cards?" Any hope that giving them the jewels would end the terror slid away. Misty nodded to her bag set in the corner. "Good girl." The leader stroked her face with his gloved hand. She jerked away from his caress, revulsion crawling over her skin. "Mikey, you and Brandon take the cards and get as much as you can." He leered back at Misty. "You better give us the correct numbers if you know what's good for you."

"I'm not stupid." She tried to keep the tremor out of her voice but failed. "I know it wouldn't be a good idea."

"BJ, I'll stay with her," Brandon argued, looking uneasy.

"I think you're forgetting who's in charge. Your sister and I are going to have ourselves a real good time while you're gone. In fact, if I were you, I wouldn't hurry."

Misty began to shake. Sheer black terror swept through her as fearful images built in her mind. She squeezed her eyes closed against the evil she saw staring at her. Suddenly Misty found herself being yanked to the side as the sound of scuffling broke out. Eyes flying open, she saw her brother fighting the leader.

"Run, Misty! No matter what, don't look back."

And then he was clutching at his chest, the arid smell of gunfire hanging heavy over them. Surprised, Brandon looked down at the blood seeping through his fingers. His knees gave way and he slumped to the ground. With an anguished cry, Misty ran back—directly into the face of evil—and gathered him in her arms.

"I'm so sorry, Misty. It all got out of hand." He gasped painfully. "I owed them so much money, I tried everything to raise it. Once they found out you were my sister, they said all I had to do was let them in. You were never meant to be here. I'd never let anyone hurt you." Brandon's voice grew fainter, his lips tinged blue.

"I know. You hang on and you can make it up to me,"

Misty pleaded, barely seeing her brother's face through the haze of tears.

"Do you forgive me?" So quiet now, she had to lean forward to catch the word.

"Of course I forgive you." Misty kissed his forehead gently. "You're my big brother. I love you." A gentle exhale left Brandon's body, as if he'd only managed to hold on long enough to hear the words. Sobbing, Misty clutched him to her, knowing he was beyond pain now.

"That got me right here." The leader thumped at his chest, wresting Brandon's body from her. Struggling to get back to her brother, she slipped in a pool of his blood. "Mikey, what are you waiting for? Go get that money." The accomplice scurried off, and Misty shivered at the pure evil she saw in the leader's eyes. "It's just you and me now."

CHAPTER 19

Once when Logan was younger, on a dare he'd draped the class python around his neck. The snake had decided to get friendlier than he'd liked, and the next minute spots had been dancing before his eyes. It had taken his teacher, the gym teacher and his friends to free him from it, and yet it had still been easier to escape that creature's clutches than one Lilian Westminster.

Logan rubbed the back of his neck, sighing as he climbed the stairs up to the grand front door. All he wanted was a long, hot shower and maybe a stiff drink. The door swung open silently on well-oiled hinges, his boots echoing on the Italian marble tiles. It was eerily quiet, like a museum or an art gallery. Maybe Misty had already gone to bed. Disappointment filled him and he took his coat off a little rougher than necessary. He'd been looking forward to regaling her with how his date had gone, maybe over a nightcap or two. Logan looked around at the blazing illumination surrounding him. It seemed like every light in the house was on. Apparently rich people didn't worry about how they were going to pay the utility bills like the rest of the mere mortals. It was only as he made his way farther into the house that the hairs on the back of his neck began to stir. *Why are the paintings all off the walls?*

A scream rent through the air. Heart-pounding fear drove him into action. *Misty!* Blindly, he ran toward the sound, praying he was going in the right direction as the terrified sound played on a loop in his mind. Her bedroom door was slightly ajar, and he heard muffled screams, like someone was holding a hand over her mouth, and the sound of a struggle. Panic like he'd never known welled in his throat as he charged the door, hitting it with his shoulder as it refused to fully open. Putting more weight behind it, whatever it was began to slowly give way, the noises from inside battering at him the whole while.

At last, he created enough of a gap to get through and discovered, to his horror, what had been blocking it. Brandon's lifeless eyes stared up at him, a dark pool blooming on the white carpet around him. The dead man's blood was smeared in a trail, mute evidence of Misty's battle to remain beside her brother. Logan's searching gaze locked on the man with his back to him who was struggling with Misty on the bed, the pristine bedsheets bloodied. *She was alive!* Terror gave way to a rage so pure it threatened to consume him.

With a roar that was torn from deep within his soul, Logan charged toward the bed, slamming a fist into the unprotected back of Misty's assailant. He was only dimly aware of her petrified eyes staring at him, unknowing yet who or what terror was happening next as the man slumped forward, unconscious from the blow. Not satisfied, Logan rolled him over off Misty and continued to pound his fist over and over, a terrible kind of rhythm settling over him. It was only when Misty's hysterical crying broke through the horrible miasma that had swallowed him whole that he stopped, jerking back in disgust at the mess of blood and bone making up what remained of the other man's face.

Logan pulled Misty's trembling form close. "It's okay, baby. It's all over." A thought too terrifying to even entertain had him holding her away from him, inspecting her bloodied clothing closely. "Are you hurt? Baby, where are you hurt?"

"It's Brandon's." Misty hiccupped through her sobs. "He's dead, Logan. He died trying to protect me."

She collapsed under the pain of her loss. Logan didn't know what else to do but hold her. His questions of why her brother was even there when he'd left that morning could wait. Pulling her into him as if he could take some of her pain away, he grimly reached for his phone and began to dial 911.

HE SEEMED SMALLER SOMEHOW, handcuffed to the stretcher as he was wheeled away. Misty wrapped her arms around herself in scant protection as the man who had killed her brother and tried to assault her left the room. Brandon's body was being carefully placed into a dark blue bag, his features slowly disappearing as it was zipped up.

"No!" she screamed, pushing the paramedics away.

Logan's arms were around her again. "Misty, I'm so sorry, baby, but you need to let them do what they need to do."

"No, he doesn't like having anything over his face. It took forever for him to learn to put his head underwater. If they cover his face, he'll be scared." She sobbed, still trying to get to her brother. "I don't want him to be scared."

"Can you please give us a minute?" Logan asked the paramedics. With sympathetic glances in her direction, they busied themselves elsewhere. "Misty, he's gone."

"I know." Her anguish almost overcame the thin control

she had. "But I only just got my brother back." A raw, primitive grief overwhelmed her. "I finally had my brother back." Misty stared down at her hands, Brandon's dried blood still on them. "I need to shower. I need to get this off me." She compulsively began to scratch at her skin, her breaths coming in short, ragged gasps. Wheezing painfully, she struggled to breathe. A paramedic, seeing her plight, quickly held Ventolin to her lips. Misty closed her eyes, concentrating on each inhale and exhale until the asthma attack passed.

With quick movements, she found herself in Logan's strong, muscular arms as he strode out of the room. "We still have more questions for her," a police officer called after them.

"And they can wait until she's clean and in fresh clothes." Logan's pace didn't slow. "Can't you see she's had enough? She just had a stress-induced asthma attack, and I'm not hanging around until she has another one."

If Misty had the capacity left to feel any emotion other than pain, she would've been surprised at the extreme care he handled her with—like delicate glass—as he set her down on her feet in the bathroom and turned on the shower. Numbly glancing around, she recognized it as the ensuite of his guest room.

"Baby, I'm going to get you some clean clothes, and then I'll be right back." Logan stared at her. On a subconscious level, she knew he was waiting for some form of acknowledgment. Jerkily, she nodded her head, holding herself rigid as he left, closing the door quietly behind him.

Misty's clothes stuck to her skin as she began to remove them, clinging to her like memories of the evening that ghosted her mind. A wall of steam billowed in her face as she opened the shower door, the humidity making the air thick. She watched the water cascading over her body turn dark as the blood swirled in crimson eddies before escaping, swirling down the drain. She'd have to call her parents. Brandon had been their child—their first born—and no matter how far from perfect he'd strayed, they'd loved him with almost a compulsion. Misty covered her face with trembling hands and gave vent to the agony of her loss.

How long she remained frozen, trapped in the vortex of her grief, she didn't know. It was only the gentle knock on the door from Logan that pulled her back to reality. "Misty, I've got some fresh clothes for you and a hairbrush. I didn't know what else to get."

"Thank you."

"Baby, they've captured the other guy who was here tonight. He was trying to purchase gas on your credit card." Strange that she hadn't thought of the other man, the one she hadn't known before tonight. Before today, he could've been just another nameless face in the crowd. "Misty, did you hear me?" Worry crept into Logan's voice.

"They got the other guy," she repeated back in a monotone, disconnected from the words.

"I'm going to open the door slightly and put your clothes just inside." Misty watched as a sliver of the world outside her steamy sanctuary appeared, a bodiless arm reaching through with the bundle of clothes before shutting her off again. "I'm staying right here outside this door. We can talk if you want, or say nothing. Whatever you want to do."

The tenderness in his voice made tears well up in Misty's eyes. Turning the water off, she grabbed a fluffy towel and began to rub her skin dry. "I don't know what to do. Losing Indie was like losing a sister, but I'd lost so much time with Brandon. It's not fair." She slipped the sweats on and opened the door. "Why?"

Misty shuffled over to the patiently waiting cowboy. Dejectedly, she sunk onto the bed beside him, Logan pulling her close. "Sometimes no matter how hard we try to run, we still have to pay the piper. What he did at the end, he made amends for everything."

In time, maybe that would be salve to her agony. But for now, Misty could see nothing but her misery. Closing her eyes, she prayed for sleep that would take her away from this reality. A reality that only Logan's strong arms buffered her from.

CHAPTER 20

All night Logan watched the gentle rise and fall of Misty's chest, the flutter of her dark lashes against her pale cheeks as if even in her dreams she couldn't escape the clutches of despair. In one moment, he could have lost the infuriating, impossibly brilliant, stubborn love of his life. He'd spent so long running away, scared that if he didn't, then she'd leave. *What a fool!*

It had been his stubborn pride. But then again, it was something she had in spades, too. *Heaven help their children.* She was the one thing in his life that was irreplaceable. Logan's blood ran cold as he thought about what could have happened if he'd stayed for one more drink, tolerated Lilian's pawing a couple of minutes longer. Well, that way lies insanity. Life had given him a warning of what he stood to lose, and he wasn't going to ignore it. Gently tucking the covers around Misty, he quietly padded to the bathroom.

A PLEASANT MUSKY fragrance tickled Misty's nose as she burrowed further into the pillow, not quite ready to leave the softness of slumber. In that moment she felt safe, oddly protected. But like a freight train, the trauma of the previous night slammed into her. She felt icy fingers of anguish seep into every pore, and a suffocating sensation clawed at her throat. Misty was conscious of a low, tortured sob, like a wounded animal. Strangely detached, she discovered it was coming from herself.

And then the musky fragrance was back, stronger than before, as Logan gathered her in his arms, crooning softly to her. "I'm sorry I left. I wanted to shower and change clothes before you woke up. I promise I won't leave you again."

Misty gave a bitter bark of laughter. "Yeah, like I can believe that." She hardened her heart against the flash of hurt she saw in his eyes. She couldn't handle any more emotion. "Isn't it almost time you left? You always do."

"This time I mean it. I've never promised to stay, but that's what I'm doing now. If you'll have me."

Old fears and uncertainty battled for space in Misty's beleaguered heart. "I don't think I can survive much more pain."

Logan kissed the top of her bowed head. "I know. Misty, I've spent most of my grown life being afraid of loving you. Turns out I'm more afraid of losing you."

A tiny glimmer of light in the otherwise darkness of her soul flickered to life. "You love me?"

"Yeah. Our kind of love is fiery and passionate with a little spice, and I wouldn't change it for the world. I just needed to grow into the man who could see it for what it was, not fear it for a maybe."

"You've broken my heart more than once, and yet it still kept wanting to love you." Misty recognized the truth in her words. "Right now, it's bruised and needs time to heal."

"I understand." Logan lifted her chin to stare into her eyes. The look in them was strong and steady, not a single glimmer of uncertainty. "I reckon there's lots to figure out, too. I'm not sure I'm cut out for your big city living, but I'll try, if that's what you want."

The fact he would offer to give up living where he was happiest filled Misty with amazement and love for this wonderfully complicated onion of a man. "I would never ask that of you. William loves the New York City lifestyle, and he's more than capable of handling the things that need someone on the ground. Truth is, I need some time to heal, and I miss Evelyn and Hope. Maybe it's time I base in Texas and only come back to work when I absolutely have to."

"Texas is good for the soul," Logan sagely replied, trying to cover a smile of pure joy that threatened to break out. "I mean, I kinda bounce between my truck and my parents and Shelby's place, but I'm sure Colt would let us crash there for a while. At least till we find something of our own."

"You've never really found a home of your own, have you?"

Her observation seemed to startle him. Logan blinked, pondering her words. "I've found it, and now I'm bringing her back to Texas with me."

Misty didn't need to answer. The truth of it was on her lips as his mouth hungrily covered hers. *Home at last.*

THE END

As an Indie Author, reviews help me get my books noticed. If you enjoyed reading Logan and Misty's story as much as I did writing it, please leave a review. It will make all the difference to me.

If you loved, *The Billionairess' Cowboy,* sign up for my newsletter here to get the free bonus's and exclusive news.

Now, turn the page to discover Shelby and William's Story,
The Billionaires' Cowgirl

SNEAK PEEK – THE BILLIONAIRE'S COWGIRL

*W*illiam would never understand, for as long as he lived, what had possessed Misty to uproot her life and leave civilization for Texas. If that wasn't bad enough, she'd invited him down to see her new ranch on the same weekend that a whiteout had hit New York City, forcing him into a completely unnecessary road trip. The fact he'd had to purchase a car to undertake said road trip spoke volumes about how he felt about driving even a short distance.

He didn't like to admit that it wasn't the same in New York since Misty had had the audacity to fall in love with that rodeo clown. Secretly, William harbored a liking for Logan. It took a special kind of man to know how to handle his business partner, and the cowboy had managed it and made her disgustingly happy to boot. It was just that now he was left feeling lonely and at loose ends in a city that never slept.

A loud knock from the engine pulled him back from his musing. William wasn't a mechanic—he barely knew one end of the car from the other, which his soft hands attested for—

but the noise seemed at odds with the usual effortless purr the supercar had displayed on the trip so far. The navigation system teasingly showed that he was under 20 miles until he was at Misty's ranch and he could tell her exactly how much she owed him for the indignity she'd forced upon him.

The knock fell silent, and William made a note to call the dealership when an almighty *kaboom* made him hit his head on the low ceiling. A cloud of black smoke trailed out from under the hood as the car ground to a halt. William pounded the palms of his hands against the wheel.

"You've got to be kidding me!"

Resigned, he pulled out his phone and began to search for the local mechanic, surprised that the shop had the same name as Misty's new beau. Erikson Mechanical Service. He knew there was a sister, but maybe Logan had a brother Misty had never mentioned. Rubbing a stinging palm on his trousers, he began to dial, praying a martini wasn't too far into his future or at this rate even a cold beer. He sniffed. *How the mighty have fallen.* And he hadn't even been in Texas for more than a couple of hours—imagine what he'd be like by the end of the week!

The Billionaire's Cowgirl available on Amazon and in Kindle Unlimited here

ACKNOWLEDGMENTS

A debt of gratitude to my editor Rebekah Groves for her patience with me.

Another big thanks to Megan from Designed with Grace for her cover design.

To my amazing beta readers and street team, you guys rock and I couldn't do it without you. Special mention to Lisa and Cair.

And finally to my fabulous alpha reader Trixie Norman, for all the late nights of reading and endless questions about your thoughts.

The prequel to the Barrels and Hearts series. True love is only the beginning….of the story. Find out where it all began with Ana and Eduardo. Sometimes finding love is easy. It's keeping it that's hard.

Buy here

A Cowgirl's Dream

An Aussie cowgirl far from home. A handsome Brazilian bull rider. Can they have a rodeo love story of their dreams?

Buy Now

A Cowgirl's Heart

An Aussie cowgirl in need. Her childhood friend to the rescue. Can friendship turn into a love story?

Buy Now

A Cowgirl's Passion

One feisty cowgirl. One steadfast Brazilian bull rider. Will she see what is right in front of her?

Buy Now

A Cowgirl's Pride

An Aussie cowgirl from the wrong side of the tracks. A handsome equine vet. Can they find a way to have their happy ever after?

Buy Now

A Cowgirl's Love

A young Aussie cowgirl. A widowed rancher. Does age matter when it comes to love?

Buy Now

A Cowgirl's Movie Star

A fiery cowgirl with big dreams. A movie star far from home. When their two worlds collide, will their love be strong enough to hold them together or will they be pulled apart

Buy Now

A Cowgirl's Billionaire

A cowgirl adrift. A broken billionaire cowboy. Can he free himself from the past to be the man she needs now?

Buy Now

Cowboy Christmas Series

The Mistletoe Collection

Boots and Mistletoe

Cowboy boots, mistletoe, and a holiday do-over…

Buy Now

The Cowboy Under the Mistletoe

It'll take more than the magic of the season to help this grump find her happily ever after…

Buy Now

Mistletoe and the Billionaire's Cowgirl

He's the last man she wants this holiday season. Too bad he's exactly what she needs…

Buy Now